THE PASSIONATE PRINCESS

Barbara Cartland

Barbara Cartland Ebooks Ltd

This edition © 2020

ISBNs

9781788672610   EPUB

9781788672627   PAPERBACK

Book design by M-Y Books
m-ybooks.co.uk

THE BARBARA CARTLAND ETERNAL COLLECTION

The Barbara Cartland Eternal Collection is the unique opportunity to collect all five hundred of the timeless beautiful romantic novels written by the world's most celebrated and enduring romantic author.

Named the Eternal Collection because Barbara's inspiring stories of pure love, just the same as love itself, the books will be published on the internet at the rate of four titles per month until all five hundred are available.

The Eternal Collection, classic pure romance available worldwide for all time .

THE LATE DAME BARBARA CARTLAND

Barbara Cartland, who sadly died in May 2000 at the grand age of ninety eight, remains one of the world's most famous romantic novelists. With worldwide sales of over one billion, her outstanding 723 books have been translated into thirty six different languages, to be enjoyed by readers of romance globally.

Writing her first book 'Jigsaw' at the age of 21, Barbara became an immediate bestseller. Building upon this initial success, she wrote continuously throughout her life, producing bestsellers for an astonishing 76 years. In addition to Barbara Cartland's legion of fans in the UK and across Europe, her books have always been immensely popular in the USA. In 1976 she achieved the unprecedented feat of having books at numbers 1 & 2 in the prestigious B. Dalton Bookseller bestsellers list.

Although she is often referred to as the 'Queen of Romance', Barbara Cartland also wrote several historical biographies, six autobiographies and numerous theatrical plays as well as books on life, love, health and cookery. Becoming one of Britain's most popular media personalities and dressed in her trademark pink, Barbara spoke on radio and television about social and political issues, as well as making many public appearances.

In 1991 she became a Dame of the Order of the British Empire for her contribution to literature and her work for humanitarian and charitable causes.

Known for her glamour, style, and vitality Barbara Cartland became a legend in her own lifetime. Best remembered for her wonderful romantic novels and loved by millions of readers worldwide, her books remain treasured for their heroic heroes, plucky heroines and traditional values. But above all, it was Barbara Cartland's overriding belief in the positive power of love to help, heal and improve the quality of life for everyone that made her truly unique.

AUTHOR'S NOTE

Hungarians are passionate, romantic and wild underneath their charming exterior. The very intensity and strength of their feelings exemplifies their characters and their outlook on life.

They are often a bewildering people to outsiders. They have an enormous capacity for enjoyment and tenacious friendships.

They are easy-going, but, once they are roused, nothing will stop them.

For a national cause a Magyar will do anything. Love of his country is impregnated into his very being and at its call he will commit himself to sublime sacrifice.

Music, like love, is in their blood. For generations the gypsies have stirred the souls of man with their music.

The *Csdrdds*, a tavern dance, originated in the nineteenth century. The gypsy beauty, the gypsy madness, the fierce passion, unutterable sadness, their love and rage, is all to be found in it.

Among the peasants, the magic of the gypsy is far more potent in cases of real need than the supernatural powers claimed by the Priests of any Church.

CHAPTER ONE
1870

Princess Thea was singing as she walked along the passage and went down a secondary staircase.

She was thinking as she did so that it was annoying that the best part of The Palace was always kept for Royal Receptions.

She had always enjoyed the pomp and circumstance of the Grand Staircase with its gilt and crystal balustrade. She loved the many pictures on the walls and the magnificent marble mantelpieces, which had been sculpted by gifted Italian craftsmen.

It was her great-grandfather who had made The Palace one of the most impressive in the whole of the Balkans.

He had felt, the Princess always thought, that it was a compensation for Kostas being, as a country, so small and comparatively unimportant compared to its neighbours.

She often thought that he had suffered from what was really an inferiority complex.

He had insisted on always being surrounded by a panoply of all the grandeur that went with Monarchy.

He had even expounded such ideas to his great-grandchildren and Princess Thea had been Christened 'Sydel Niobe Anthea'.

She had, however, repudiated such a mouthful of a name from the moment she could speak.

She liked referring to herself as 'Thea'. The name had then stuck and so no one in the family had called her anything else.

She went into the breakfast room.

It was a quite a pleasant and cheerful room but not impressive except that caught the morning sun.

She found her brother, Georgi, having his breakfast and reading the morning newspaper.

He looked up as his sister came into the room and called out,

"You are late!"

"Yes, I know," Thea replied, "but it was so lovely this morning and Mercury took all the jumps as if he was flying."

She then helped herself to one of the dishes of what was a very English breakfast on the sideboard.

Her father, King Alpheus of Kostas, had spent quite a lot of time when he was a young man in England.

He had actually taken a degree at Oxford University on the subject of history. And he had therefore imitated many English ways and insisted that his children spoke fluent English.

This was not difficult for Thea and Georgi as they had studiously learnt the languages of all the surrounding Balkan countries.

Georgi had once commented that, after some of them, English was 'a piece of cake'.

Carrying her plate, Thea then sat down at the table.

Her mind was still on her ride and, as she picked up her knife and fork, she said,

"By the way, Georgi, the fences should be higher."

"I know that," her brother replied. "You had better see to it."

"Why me?"

"I am going away tomorrow."

"Going away?" his sister exclaimed. "But why and where are you going?"

Georgi looked over his shoulder in case one of the footmen might hear what he was about to say and then he began to explain,

"As it happens, Thea, I am going to Paris. But you must not tell Mama. She thinks I am paying a semi-State Visit to the French Army in Arras."

"You are going to Paris again?" Thea queried him. "I cannot think why you don't stay here for a while."

Her brother smiled.

"I can give you just one answer to that, Paris is extremely amusing and the women are fantastic!"

Thea stared at him.

"You mean you are just going to France to enjoy yourself?"

"That about sums it up in a nutshell."

"And you are going – alone?"

"I shall not be alone for long!"

"Take me with you! Please take me with you," Thea started to plead with him.

"You can hear Mama agreeing to that," Georgi scoffed.

"But surely we could say that I was staying with one of your friends?"

"Mama would certainly not approve."

"Why not?"

"Because the Paris wmen are fascinating and very attractive, but certainly not the right companions for a well-brought-up Princess like you!"

Thea made a sound of disgust.

"Why could I not have been a boy?"

"You will find that quite a lot of men will be glad you are a girl!"

Thea looked at him derisively.

"Men?" she asked him. "Where do I ever see them, except for the old Courtiers who are practically falling into the grave?"

Her brother poured himself out another cup of coffee.

"You have a point there," he said. "But, as it happens, Papa is arranging your marriage. He was talking to me about it last night."

Now Thea was stunned.

"My – marriage?" she repeated in a low voice.

"You are eighteen and Papa believes that you must enhance the international standing of our country by a alliance with one of our more distinguished neighbours."

"Who?" Thea asked abruptly.

"It seems likely to be King Otho of Kanaris."

There was a horrified silence until Thea asked him, "Are – you – serious?"

"There does not appear to be anyone else."

"But he is old – much older than – Papa!"

"His country is twice the size of ours."

"But – how can I possibly – marry an old man like that? When I saw him last his hair and his beard were – white!"

"It's a bit hard on you," her brother did concede, "but – you have to marry someone."

"I-I want to marry someone young – who I am deeply – in love with."

Georgi sat back in his chair.

"You know just as well as I do, Thea, because we are Royal, we have to take what is available and think of our country first and ourselves last!"

"If that is what you really think, then why do you not marry?" Thea enquired.

There was a poignant silence for a moment.

And then her brother admitted,

"I know it has to happen sometime and Papa is already looking around. She is sure to be plain, fat and deadly dull!"

He spoke violently and then added,

"That is why I want to go to Paris. I intend to enjoy myself while I can."

There was a distinct harshness in the way he spoke.

Then she asked him in a small voice,

"Must – I do – this?"

"You know the answer to that perfectly well," her brother replied.

"There must be – somebody better than – King Otho!"

"That is what I said to Papa last night, but he pointed out that practically every one of our neighbours is either married with six children or a widower like King Otho or a misogynist like King Árpád.

"What is a misogynist?" Thea enquired.

"A man who hates women," her brother answered. "It usually happens when a man has had an unfortunate love affair, which leaves him cynical and bitter about women."

"But – there must be – someone else!" Thea almost shouted desperately.

"I am sorry, old girl, but I did go through all the possibilities with Papa and we came up with nothing."

"It's so unfair!" Thea cried. "I will not – marry him! I shall – refuse."

She spoke very violently, but she well knew in her heart that, if there was no acceptable alternative, it was something that she would have to do.

She was perfectly aware that her father's obsession with improving the status of Kostas would make him obstinate. So nothing she could say would have any effect on him.

She stared across the table at Georgi and there were now tears in her eyes as she pleaded,

"Help me – Georgi – *please* – help me!"

"I only wish I could," Georgi replied, "but I am in the same boat as you are. I shall be twenty-two next month and Papa has told me that I have to be married by next year and start to provide more heirs to the Throne."

Thea rose from the breakfast table and then murmured to herself,

'The whole – idea makes me feel sick.'

She walked to the window to look out at the well-laid out garden that was bright with colourful spring flowers.

What she was really seeing, however, was the lined face of King Otho and his white hair growing thin on the top of his head.

She had never imagined and never thought for one single moment that she would be forced to marry a man like him.

Because she had been so much alone when Georgi was at school and then in the Army, she read as many Fairy stories as she could find.

She believed them and they became part of her very existence.

She had dreamt that one day a tall handsome Prince would suddenly come into her life.

They would fall instantly in love, be married and live happily ever after.

He would understand how much the beauty of the countryside meant to her and the high mountains with snowy peaks that enclosed Kostas as well as the silver river that ran through the valley and fed the verdant fields on either side of it.

The peasants were indeed poor, but there was always plenty of fruit and vegetables and the women were noted for their lovely skins.

Kostas lay on the Southern border of Hungary and their blood had been mixed over the centuries, which accounted for many of the women having red hair that was characteristic of the Hungarians.

Thea's hair was red, but it was not the dark auburn shade that was common in Austria. It was rather a mixture of red and gold, which in the sunshine made her hair seem like dancing flames.

It was inevitable that her eyes should be green and, when she was upset, they seemed to have a dark almost purple tinge in them.

She had no idea that her brother was now watching her closely.

He was thinking how Thea had in the last year developed into a beauty and there was no doubt that she would grow even lovelier as she grew older.

It was a pity that there was no one more suitable for her as a husband than King Otho, but there was, however, nothing he could do about it.

He had in point of fact done his best. He had argued with his father until in exasperation the King had said,

"Don't be more of a fool than you are usually, Georgi. We are not important enough to be considered seriously by the Royalty of larger countries!"

His voice was harsh as he added,

"Nor has Thea a large enough dowry to attract them."

Georgi was fully aware that this was always a sore point that his father had never had as much money as he required.

This was partly due to the ambitious schemes of his father, who had spent an inordinate amount of money building The Palace and laying out the extensive grounds.

He had also provided their small Army with colourful and elaborate uniforms as well as up to date guns that they never used.

Unless they found gold in the mountains or pearls in the river, which was most unlikely, Georgi knew that they would have to struggle on trying to make ends meet.

He was therefore aware that his father was looking for a Princess with plenty of money for him.

It did not matter whether she was fat, thin, plain or pretty, if her dowry was big enough, he would have to accept her.

It was the dreadful thought of being saddled with such a wife that had made Georgi rush off to Paris.

There the fascinating *courtesans* might well be expensive, but they knew how to make a man forget. He was thinking of just how enjoyable it had been the last time he had visited that fabulous City.

He knew that there were several alluring *filles de joie* who would welcome him back to Paris with open arms.

It was not only because he was a Prince or that somehow he managed to pay them.

He was an extremely good-looking young man. What was more the men of Kostas were noted for being fascinating and ardent lovers.

This too was something that they had inherited from Hungary and the fact that they were brilliant horsemen as well.

Georgi rose from his chair and walked towards his sister.

He put his arm comfortingly around her shoulders and said,

"Cheer up, old girl! When we are both married, I will make some excuse to take you to Paris or perhaps even to England with me."

Thea was listening intently and he added,

"A married woman has far more licence than a young girl."

"I want to – come with – you now."

"I wish I could take you," Georgi replied, "but I expect you would be shocked and it would considerably cramp my style!"

Thea accepted this and then she asked in a very small voice,

"You – you don't think that Papa – would do – anything while – you are away?"

"If I have the chance, I will persuade him not to," Georgi promised. "At the same time I don't want him to make it an excuse to cancel my trip."

Thea gave a deep sigh.

"No – of course not."

"What you have to do," her brother went on, "is to enjoy yourself while you can. Raise the fences and ride while you still don't have to be accompanied everywhere."

Thea gasped.

"Do you mean – if I am married – I shall have to have some – dreary Lady-in-Waiting or *aide-de-camp* with me?"

Georgi did not reply and she knew the answer already.

Of course as a Queen she would be hedged around as if she was a prisoner.

They were somewhat understaffed at The Palace and she therefore had been allowed to ride alone in the Park without having a groom always in attendance.

It was understood that she did not go outside the high walls that encircled the Park. There she could be alone, she could think and she could talk to Mercury without being overheard.

Now she began to consider the ultimate horror of being so important that she could never be alone.

It would be different, she thought, if she could ride with someone she loved. Someone she could talk to and laugh with.

In the stories that she told herself, her dream man, who was naturally Prince Charming, was always a magnificent rider.

They would ride stallions that were so fine and so spirited that no one could keep up with them.

Then they would ride away alone into the light of an infinite horizon.

Thinking of King Otho, she felt quite certain that he was not a good rider and most certainly not an outstanding one.

She was sure that he would also be very particular about protocol and endless Court ritual.

She had tried not to listen to her Governesses when they had said to her,

"A Princess does not do this – a Princess does not do that! You must remember, Your Royal Highness, that you are a Princess."

Now she was certain that the same would be said by her husband.

It would be exactly the same routine, except that it would be,

"A Queen does not do anything she wants to do."

As if Georgi knew what she was thinking, he gave her a hug and said,

"I have to go now. I am accompanying Papa on a Parade that is exactly like the one he took last week and the week before that."

"But you will be free tomorrow?" Thea asked.

"Thank God for small mercies!" her brother replied. "Even though, as you well know, they are very small and very short."

He walked out of the breakfast room as he spoke, but Thea did not follow him.

Instead she continued to look blindly out of the window and every part of her body was crying out in horror.

When finally she went to the music room where her teacher was waiting for her, she was very pale.

Her Governesses had been dispensed with as soon as she had reached the magical age of eighteen and there were, however, certain Teachers who came from outside The Palace and with them she continued her studies.

Her absolute favourite of them all was the old Professor who taught her music.

He had been a great success all over Europe playing with famous orchestras before he had retired.

It was the Queen who had been clever enough to realise that he could be just the right sort of Teacher for her daughter.

The Professor taught Thea to express herself in the way she played the piano and in the compositions that she wrote.

She tried to translate into her music the beauty that made her heart leap when she looked at anything really lovely and inspiring.

She listened to the sounds of the birds and then she expressed on the piano, the joy of life in their voices.

When she went into the music room, the Professor was sitting at the piano and he was playing a soft dreamy waltz that was very romantic.

It made Thea think of the Prince Charming that she had believed one day she would find.

Then, with an almost brutal sense of stark reality, she then remembered that he was King Otho!

The Professor greeted her and she sat down at the piano.

She then began to play of the terror, misery and sense of revolt that she felt at what was waiting for her.

*

It was not until the evening that Thea received a message from her father.

His Chief *aide-de-camp* was a middle-aged man who had served the King faithfully for many years.

He knocked on the door politely and then came into her sitting room to say,

"His Majesty has asked me to inform Your Royal Highness that he wishes to see you in his study."

Thea had been reading one of her favourite magazines and thought almost clairvoyantly that this was the moment of Doom.

She had prayed that her father would delay what he had to say to her until Georgi had returned from Paris and she had clung to her brother's assurance that he would ask him to do so.

She was aware now that, because the King was always impatient, he wanted to get on with the whole arrangement.

'Before I know where I am,' she reflected, 'I shall be up the aisle and married.'

She wondered if she could tell the *aide-de-camp* that she was too tired and too unwell to obey her father's summons.

Then she knew that, if she did so, she would be unable to ride tomorrow.

Mercury would be waiting for her as usual and she thought wildly that only her horse would understand exactly what she was feeling.

"I also have to report to Your Royal Highness," the *aide-de-camp* was saying, "that Prince Georgi changed his plans at the last moment and has decided to leave for Paris this evening."

"You mean – he has already – gone?" Thea asked in astonishment.

"His Royal Highness only just had time to catch the Express. And he asked me to say 'goodbye' to you, Your Royal Highness."

Without being told Thea knew exactly what had happened.

Georgi had asked their father to do nothing about her marriage until he returned.

The King had refused and her brother had therefore run away from the problem.

She knew that he heartily disliked any sort of scene, especially recriminations, and so he had taken the easy way out and she did not blame him.

She only realised that he had accepted the inevitable and he knew that there was nothing he could do about it.

Slowly she put down her magazine and rose wearily to her feet.

"Please tell His Majesty that I will be with him – in a few minutes."

The *aide-de-camp* bowed and left the room, closing the door quietly behind him.

Thea then walked to where hanging on the wall was a mirror in an elaborate gold frame surmounted by cupids.

She stared at her reflection.

Then she took a deep breath and asked aloud,

"Mirror, mirror, tell me true. Help me, tell me what to do!"

She almost expected the mirror to reply to her, but instead there was only the reflection of herself.

Her small oval face, her straight little nose and her large green eyes and the last light of the setting sun was now turning her hair to flaming gold.

Then, with a sound that was half a groan and half a sob, she turned from the mirror and went out of the room and down the stairs.

Her father's study was a extremely comfortable room. Unlike the gilt-foamed, tapestry-covered furniture in the main part of The Palace, the King had big and comfortable leather armchairs.

The sofa was as soft as a feather bed and there was a large flat-topped desk that was easy to write on.

The pictures around the room were all of his ancestors and their frames were carved and gilded and each one was surmounted by a gold crown. There were also, because the King appreciated them, some fine Chinese vases and in each there was an arrangement of purple and white lilac together with syringa.

The whole room, Thea had frequently thought, expressed the many different facets of her father's character.

At the same time she was aware that it was impossible not to look at the enormous Royal Insignia carved and painted in gold and brilliant colours that hung over the mantelpiece.

Sitting at his desk the King would look directly at the Royal Insignia.

She thought that they would remind him every day, every hour and every minute of his responsibilities towards his Kingdom and its people.

As Thea entered the study, her father was standing with his back to the mantelpiece.

"Good evening, my dear," he greeted her. "I have been very busy all day, but now I want to talk to you."

Thea kissed his cheek and that sat down on the sofa.

She clasped her hands tightly together and was fully aware of what was coming.

"You are now eighteen," the King began, "and we have to think about your future."

"I am very happy as I am, Papa."

"I am very happy to have you with me here at the Palace," the King said. "At the same time your mother was only eighteen when we were married."

Thea was just about to say,

'To a man *only* five years older than herself.'

Then she realised that to do so would be to betray Georgi's confidence and her father would find out that he had already told her about King Otho.

"I have been thinking who would best help our beloved country," the King went on, "if they had a close alliance with us."

He paused as if he expected Thea to speak and, when she did not do so, he continued,

"As it happens, I had a letter this morning from King Otho, asking if he might come here in four days' time."

Thea drew in her breath and clenched her fingers until the knuckles were white.

"I have the idea," her father continued, "that he had almost clairvoyantly realised what I have been thinking."

"What – is that – Papa?" Thea asked him hesitantly.

Her voice did not sound in any way like her own.

"An alliance between Otho's country and ours would be very advantageous for us."

He glanced at his daughter before he added,

"I have therefore sent a reply to tell him how warmly he will be welcomed here and how much we are looking forward to his visit."

"Are you – saying, Papa," Thea then asked, "that you think – King Otho would – make me a – suitable husband?"

"You would be Queen of a large and prosperous country and in that position I am sure that you could help Kostas in a thousand different ways."

Thea felt as if her legs had given way and she would not be able to walk.

"I-I am sorry, Papa – but I – cannot marry King Otho."

"What did you say?" her father asked.

"H-he is old – much too old for me! And – if I do marry – I wish to be – in love."

"What do you mean – if you *do* marry?" the King asked. "Of course you have to marry! It is your duty to do so."

"But not to a man who is – old enough to be – my father."

"Old? What has age to do with it?" the King demanded. "He is a King and you will be a Queen!"

His voice was sharp, but Thea replied,

"I want to – love the man I – marry."

"Love? Love?" the King said. "That is all young women think about. Well, in my mind there is every reason to believe that you will grow to love your husband."

"How can you be – sure of – that?" Thea asked him.

With an effort the King then tried to be conciliatory.

"You are very young, my dear, and you must therefore allow me to know what is best for you. I feel sure that Otho will always be kind and treat you with propriety."

"But – I want to be – loved!" Thea persisted.

"Love will come after marriage," the King answered firmly.

"How can you be sure?" Thea asserted. "If I don't find him attractive now, why should he be any different just because I have his ring on my finger?"

Her father hesitated and she sensed that he was finding it difficult to explain in words what he was thinking.

There was quite a long silence.

Then Thea rose to her feet.

"I am really sorry, Papa, but I will not – marry King Otho and – it would – then be a – mistake to let him come – here under false pretences."

The King glared at her.

"Are you teaching me how to behave?" he shouted angrily. "Good God, most girls would be thrilled at the prospect of becoming a reigning Queen!"

"Not with a man as old as King Otho," Thea retorted.

"What does it matter is he is old or young?"

"It matters to me! *I* have to marry him – not you!"

The King then lost his temper.

"How dare you speak to me like that?" he roared. "You will do as you are told and I will have no nonsense about it!"

"What will you do?" Thea asked. "Drag me to the Altar unconscious? I swear I will not say the words that will make me – his wife!"

Her father now went crimson in the face.

"*Dammit!*" he screamed. "You are enough to try the patience of a Saint! You will do as you are told, Thea, and that is my last word on the subject."

He looked at his daughter as he spoke and realised that she was still defying him.

She was small and fragile-looking, yet at the moment there was a strange resemblance between them.

They were both completely determined to have their own way.

"*You will marry the King!*"

The words from her father's lips seemed to echo round the room.

"I will not – Papa! I completely and absolutely – refuse!"

"Very well," the King said, "unless you change your mind within the next twenty-four hours, you will be confined to your room and will have nothing to eat but bread and water."

Thea glared back at him as he went on,

"You will not be allowed to ride and your horse, Mercury, will be sold at the Horse Fair that takes place in two days time!"

The blood seemed to drain away from Thea's face.

"Did you – say," she asked, "that you would – sell Mercury?"

"I am a man of my word," the King stipulated. "Unless you consent to marry King Otho, Mercury will be sold."

For a moment Thea just stood there staring at him.

Then with a cry of a small animal caught in a trap, she turned and ran from the room.

*

Thea ran up the stairs and went into her bedroom. She closed the door and locked it.

Then, as she threw herself down on the bed, she burst into a flood of tears.

She cried helplessly, knowing that her father had won.

She loved Mercury, who had been hers ever since he was born and she loved him in many ways more than she loved her own family.

He was a part of her, he belonged to her and it was just impossible, she thought, to live without him.

For a moment she actively hated her father. He was using the one weapon that he knew would render her powerless to defy him.

She felt helplessly that she would marry the Devil himself rather than think of Mercury belonging to anyone else.

He might be ill-treated, starved or beaten and she would be unable to prevent it.

He would not understand, he would not know what had happened to him.

'I shall have to marry King Otho!'

She felt as if a demon was bending over her and he was forcing her to humiliate herself by accepting her father's decision.

She lay crying on her bed until there was a knock on the door.

"What is it?" she asked.

"It's Martha, Your Royal Highness, it's time you dressed for dinner."

"I am too ill to go down to dinner," Thea replied.

"Very well, Your Royal Highness, I'll tell them to send your dinner upstairs."

Martha then went away.

It was a question, Thea now thought, of whether she was given what everybody else was having for dinner or bread and water.

She now knew that her father would be well aware that he had won the battle. He had conquered her and she was obliged, like a slave at his chariot wheel, to obey his orders.

She would marry King Otho and it would be a grand Wedding and everyone in the City would throng the streets, cheering, waving and showering her with rose petals.

Waiting in the Cathedral for her would be an old white-haired man.

He had buried his first wife and now was marrying again, Thea was sure, simply because he wanted an heir.

It was then that she felt herself shudder. It was with a repugnance that was greater than anything that she had felt before.

She had no idea what happened when a man and a woman made love to each other, but she knew, of course, that when people were married they slept in the same bed.

King Otho would be sleeping beside her and so he would touch her with his old blue-veined hands.

She supposed that he would kiss her and she felt herself scream at the thought of his thin lips touching hers.

"I cannot bear it – *I cannot!*"

The tears were running down her cheeks.

Then she was thinking again of Mercury and seeing in her mind how well he had taken the jumps this morning.

And how he always nuzzled against her when she went to the stables and how he would come when she called him.

Mercury! *Mercury?* How could she bear to lose him?

She walked to the window and stood gazing out over the garden

Now because it was still spring, the sun had already sunk and the sky was crimson and gold on the horizon.

The last rays of the sun lingered on the snow on the mountain peaks and high overhead the first evening star twinkled in the sky.

It was so beautiful and inspiring that, despite her misery and distress, Thea felt that it lifted her heart.

On earth life might well be horrifying, degrading and revolting, but high above her was Heaven if only she could reach it.

She thought of how Apollo had driven his magnificent horses across the sky and he had brought light to those who were in darkness.

It was the light that lifted not only their hearts but also their minds.

She pictured herself riding in the same way across the sky on Mercury and then, as she visualised herself galloping into the crimson and gold of the sun as it sank lower and lower, she had an idea.

An idea so stupendous and so revolutionary that she could for a moment hardly grasp it.

With a cry she flung up her arms and she was reaching out to the stars overhead.

They had given her an answer and had brought a shining light to her mind.

"I will do it!" she cried aloud. "That is what I will do!"

CHAPTER TWO

Thea lay on her bed in the darkness thinking out her plan in detail.

She would take Mercury and disappear until after King Otho had departed.

Her father would be furiously angry, but it would take him considerable time to set up another State Visit.

She was well aware that a visiting Monarch from another country expected an enormous amount of kow-towing, special banquets and Receptions from his hosts.

She had always found that all this pompous and stiff protocol was incredibly dull and such occasions, however, always delighted her father and gave him a chance to show off what Kostas could really do.

Now, as soon as dinner was finished, he would go to his study to make his plans first for the Reception for King Otho at the frontier and then there would be a series of what Thea thought of as 'charades' to impress him.

The Army, such as it was, would be on full dress Parade and canons would be fired as a respectful Royal Salute.

Everything would be leading up to the moment when her engagement would be formally announced.

'I will – not do – it! I *will* – *not*!' she murmured to herself hundreds of times to give herself courage.

She knew only too well that she was being outrageous and revolutionary and her father would be totally appalled by her behaviour and disobedience to him and his orders.

It would, however, she thought, give him a sharp and salutary jolt to realise that she had a will of her own.

Equally she felt helpless for the moment. If she rode away, where could she go and, what was more important than anything else, she had no money.

She thought about this for some time and then jumped out of her bed and went to the window to look up at the stars.

"You have to help me," she said, "you *must* guide me!"

She remembered how a star had guided the Three Wise Men on their way to Bethlehem and that was what she needed now.

Almost as if in answer to her prayers, she recalled something that she had forgotten.

She had no ready money because she never needed it. If she went out shopping, the bills were always sent on to The Palace.

If she wished to purchase something in the market place or to give a few small coins to a beggar, it was always supplied by her Lady-in-Waiting, who invariably accompanied her on such occasions.

It had never struck her until now that she was penniless and it was an uncomfortable and disorienting feeling.

Then she was certain that it was the stars that suddenly reminded her that she did have some money.

Ever since her birth, one of her eminent Godfathers, an Archduke, gave her a present every Christmas of a golden coin of the highest denomination in Kostas.

Each bore the date of the year that he had presented it to her.

She therefore had eighteen of such gold coins and they constituted a sum of money that fortunately would pay for everything she needed a dozen times over.

She thought then that she would take ten of the coins from where she kept her special treasures.

That was the red cabinet in her sitting room and besides the gold coins there was a very pretty snuffbox that Georgi had bought for her as a present the last time he was in Paris.

There was a necklace made of seashells and she had strung them together years ago when she had been taken for a holiday by the sea.

There was also a necklace made of cherry stones, which she had been given by one of the gypsies.

The gypsies passed through Kostas usually in the summer and, because her father was a kindly and generous man, unlike some of the other reigning

Monarchs in the region, he had always welcomed them.

They had always fascinated Thea and she often went and talked to them and they taught her a little of their Romany tongue.

One of the young girls had once shown her a necklace of cherry stones.

"This, Your Royal Highness," she had said, "is magic."

"In what way?" Thea had asked her.

"When a gypsy girl sees a man who she wants to fall in love with her," the gypsy had answered, "she collects as many cherry stones as the years of her age. She then drills a hole through one stone each night beginning with the night of the new moon."

"What happens then?" Thea enquired.

"She continues drilling for three full moons and then she sleeps for thirteen nights with the necklace wound around her left knee."

Thea was listening intently to the gypsy who went on,

"When the necklace has won her a proposal of marriage from the man she loves, she keeps it for the rest of her life."

She looked at Thea as she said,

"I won the man whom I loved and he loves me. You keep this necklace, Your Royal Highness, and it will show you how to make magic when you really need it."

Thea thanked her and she had taken the necklace home and put it in her cabinet with her other treasures.

Now she took it out and held it in her hands.

'Help me to find a man I can love and who will love me,' she prayed.

Then she put it back in the case.

Now she picked out ten of the gold coins and put them in her pocket.

She was certain that ten of the most recent years would be easy to replace, but the eight earlier ones, which bore her grandfather's head, might be more difficult.

Anyway she now had some money and that was essential for her plan.

She went back into her bedroom and packed all that she intended to take with her and she would have to carry everything in a roll attached to the back of Mercury's saddle.

So it would have to be light and she chose one of the muslin gowns and thought that she would change into it in the evenings.

She added a clean white blouse, a blue nightgown and a few small things that were to her indispensable.

She packed it all in a large woollen shawl which would be warm enough to cover her shoulders if she was cold and it would also have to act as a dressing gown.

A pair of satin slippers would, she knew, go into the pocket of the saddle along with her hairbrush and comb.

Then there was a small bag containing her soap, her toothbrush, a sponge and a flannel and she wrapped all these in a chiffon scarf.

She next tried to think if there was anything else that she may require.

Then, leaving everything ready on a chair, she climbed into bed.

She did not expect to sleep, but she was tired and slept dreamlessly almost as soon as her head touched the pillow.

*

Thea awoke with a start.

It flashed through her mind that she had overslept and it would spoil her plan of escape.

Then she remembered that she had been gazing at the stars when she had climbed into bed and had left the curtains drawn back.

It had been the dawn that had awakened her and the first pale fingers of light were now creeping up the sky.

For the moment the stars were still shining brightly overhead and then Thea could see that they would soon begin to fade.

But before they did so she wished to be on her way as she glanced at the clock on the mantelpiece and saw that it was just after four o'clock in the morning.

It took her only a few minutes to dress. She had put on one of her prettiest habits, which actually matched the green of her eyes.

Her mother had refused to be interested in the new, tight-fitting riding habits that had just come into modern fashion, having been introduced by Elizabeth the Empress of Austria, who was also Queen of Hungary.

Thea's habit was very becoming. It had a full skirt and she wore with it a thin muslin blouse under a tight-fitting jacket and under her skirt were two white petticoats edged with lace.

Her riding boots reached only to her knees and with the habit went a riding hat that had a high crown and was encircled with a thin gauze veil that floated out behind her when she galloped.

This morning, however, Thea was not in the least interested in her appearance.

She dressed quickly, sweeping her long red hair round her head and she fixed it in place with hairpins.

She looked at her hat and then decided not to take it with her.

When she rode alone in the Park at The Palace, she always went hatless and occasionally her mother would warn her,

"Do be careful, dearest, of the sun. It would be very unbecoming if you had brown skin with your coloured hair."

But Thea was fortunate. The Fairies at her Christening had given her a white skin that was impervious to the sun.

"Your skin is like magnolia," somebody had remarked to her once and she realised that it was the truth.

There was also something translucent about her skin that made her glow like a pearl.

However there was nobody in The Palace who would dare to compliment her and so in consequence she had no idea of how lovely she looked.

Because she was excited, her eyes were shining and she typified the joy of spring.

She put a clean handkerchief into her pocket and remembered to pack two more in her luggage.

Pausing for a moment she wondered if she should write a letter to her father.

Then she decided that it would be a mistake.

It would be best for her to just disappear.

That she had done so would gradually percolate through The Palace as the servants could not be stopped talking and their gossiping would inevitably become exaggerated and then spread throughout the country.

When Martha found that she was not in her bedroom, she would automatically assume that she had gone riding.

When she did not come back for breakfast, she doubted if anyone would actually notice.

Her father was used to her being late in the morning and it was the only meal when the servants did not wait as the family would always help themselves.

They would most probably think that she had come and gone.

Much later in the morning, her mother, who always rose late, might be told that she was not in The Palace.

The Queen would not be perturbed, thinking that as usual she was out riding on Mercury.

It might easily be as late as luncheontime before anyone would seriously question her whereabouts.

'And by that time,' Thea mused with some considerable satisfaction, 'I shall be miles and miles away!'

Holding her two bundles tightly in her hands she peeped out through the door into the passage outside.

There appeared to be no one about.

On tiptoe she hurried to a back staircase that led to the door into the garden.

It was the one that she and Georgi always used when they had no wish to be seen or encounter either of their parents. If they did, they were more than likely to be given a task that they did not want.

Thea reached the garden door and unlocked it.

As she stepped out, the air was fresh, clean and fragrant with the scent of flowers. She slipped silently through the garden like a ghost.

When she reached the stables, there was a groom on duty. He was a young lad and was asleep on a bundle of hay.

Thea woke him by touching his arm.

"Sorry, Your Royal Highness, I just dozed off, I did!"

"That is all right," Thea smiled. "I am early as I could not sleep. Please saddle Mercury for me."

"Right you are, Your Royal Highness," the boy replied and hurried to the stall where Mercury was stabled.

As soon as the horse saw Thea, he nuzzled her and she made a fuss of him and stroked him all the time he was being saddled.

The stable boy led him out into the yard and Thea climbed onto the mounting block. She had trained Mercury to stand steady while she seated herself in the saddle.

As she did so, she said to the stable boy as he handed her the reins,

"Will you fix this onto Mercury's saddle for me?"

She gave him her shawl and he attached the ribbons that she had bound it with to the saddle loops.

Then Thea quickly put the other small bundle into the pocket of the saddle.

She knew that the stable boy would not think it strange that she should carry something at the back and, if it rained or was cold, she often took a coat with her.

He was not very intelligent, but he might, however, think it unusual that she was taking so much with her.

She waited until the boy had finished as Mercury showed his impatience by twitching his ears and tossing his head.

Then, when the stable boy smiled at her, Thea said, "Thank you very much."

"Have a nice ride then, Your Royal Highness." the stable boy replied and touched his forelock.

She rode off, deliberately not hurrying and only when she was in the Park and out of sight of The Palace did she make Mercury start moving quickly.

There was just one way that she could leave The Palace grounds without passing through a gate that was guarded by sentries.

All the main entrances had soldiers on duty, although Thea suspected that they did not exert themselves unduly at any of them.

There was, however, one very minor gate, which was used only by farm carts and the animals that came in to graze from the Home Farm.

Because it was of no importance there was nobody on guard at this gate.

Although it was supposed to be securely locked at night, Thea doubted if this always happened.

She, however, had no intention of dismounting to find out.

The gate was quite a low one and the ground around it dry and sandy.

Mercury brilliantly cleared it with at least a foot to spare.

Now Thea found herself outside the Royal fence that had hedged her in ever since she could remember.

She had often ridden down to the valley, but had never been allowed to do so alone.

If nothing else, she thought, this was indeed a new experience.

She settled down to ride quickly but carefully as she must not encounter anyone who would recognise her.

This meant that she had to be as far away as possible from The Palace before it was light.

The dawn was now forcing back the sable of the sky and the stars were fading one by one and soon the sun would come up.

What she had to do was to cross the river before other people were doing the same.

She knew already that numbers of peasants always came in early in the morning from the country to Gyula, the Capital of Kostas.

Some of them would be in carts loaded with vegetables for the market and others would be carrying what they intended to sell on their backs.

Then there would be the women who came in from the country every day to work in the City and Thea had often seen them and thought how colourful they looked.

They were in National costume, which, as in all the Balkan countries, had traditionally a red skirt, a prettily embroidered blouse and a black velvet corset that was laced down the front.

The Kostasians were a happy and outward people. They would be laughing and singing as they walked along the road.

When they saw either Thea or Georgi, they would wave excitedly and call out greetings in their musical voices.

Thea then reached the bridge and found to her considerable relief that there was no one crossing on it.

It was also far too early for anyone to be out working in the fields or to be driving their animals over the open land beyond that stretched to the foot of the mountains.

The mountains were for the moment her main objective.

She needed to cross over the plain in front of her to reach them and it was very like the Steppes of Hungary and covered with thick grass filled with wild flowers and humming bees.

It was a perfect place for Mercury to stretch his legs in a wild gallop.

He did not have to be told what to do and Thea thought that she had never moved so quickly on his back.

By the time she had ridden for a mile or two the sun had risen over the horizon and its rays, warm and golden, lit the world.

The butterflies, white and colourful, were hovering over the wild flowers. The birds were singing and the mist had risen from the river.

To Thea it was all the beauty that she had ever sought in her life and it was the beauty of her dreams.

She did not know where she was going.

She believed that last night the stars had told her to escape and now she would be guided by the sun.

'I am – free! *I am – free!*' she told herself happily

Mercury then slowed down from a gallop to an easy trot.

She looked back and she had come even further than she had expected.

There was no sign of Gyula and nothing to be seen of The Palace that rose higher than the City.

'I am free!' she murmured to herself again and wondered where she should go now.

She rode on until she realised that she was in a part of the country where she had never been before. Now there was no sign of the river nor were there any cultivated fields.

There were just the flowers and the butterflies and to her right and straight ahead were the looming mountains.

She knew, however, that there were many passes through them and some were regularly utilised and some were not.

She had never had a chance to explore them.

When she went riding outside The Palace grounds, either with her father or Georgi, there always had come the moment when they said,

"We should be going back or we will be late for luncheon."

Then again if they rode in the afternoon, they had to return in plenty of time for dinner, which was always a very formal meal.

Thea rode on for an hour or so before she thought that she was beginning to feel hungry.

She remembered that later in the day she would have to find somewhere to stay the night.

She knew that there were small lodging houses or hotels where visitors to Kostas stayed, especially those who enjoyed climbing.

It was something that Georgi had attempted and he only gave it up after he had fallen and broken his arm.

There were also sportsmen who came to Kostas to shoot the chamois and others stalked the stags, the wild goats and the wolves.

Her father always talked about them rather scathingly, but there were woven fur rugs and stag horns in The Palace that proclaimed his prowess with a rifle when he was younger.

'There must be a small hotel around here,' Thea told herself.

For the moment there was no hurry and after riding on for a few miles she drew a little nearer to the mountains.

Then she saw a pass rising higher than the land that she was riding on and there was a rough track leading up to it.

Because she felt that it would be a good place to hide, she rode Mercury up the track.

Nearer the top with the rocks rising on either side of her, she turned to look back.

She realised at once that she had come a very long way from The Palace.

If her father sent out soldiers to look for her, it would take days for them to search in the mountains.

She rode on up the pass, which could only be negotiated on horseback or on foot, but the track was narrow and not very long.

As it ended, she then found herself in a forest of fir trees, which were so thick that the sunshine could hardly percolate through them.

Thea loved the woods feeling that they were mysterious and filled with dragons and elves.

She had read everything she could find about Sylvanus, the Roman God of the Trees and she had often thought of him when she rode in the wood behind The Palace.

But that was very different from the trees that she was riding through now, which were thick dark fir trees that had grown very tall because they were reaching towards the light.

They were strange and, Thea thought, definitely part of her Fairy story.

Suddenly there was an opening in the trees and she saw to her surprise a small lake with oak trees lining each side of it and the sunshine glittered dazzlingly on the water.

And she was entranced because, as she drew Mercury to a halt, she could see the snow-topped mountains above her.

At the same time she saw a profusion of yellow irises growing on the sides of the lake and it was so lovely that she would not have been in the least surprised if she had seen a water nymph swimming in the water.

She was sure that Mercury would be thirsty now, so she rode him down to the water's edge and then dismounted.

Before she did so, she knotted his reins and then, leaving him to drink as much as he wanted she walked on, gazing at the lake, the flowers and the trees.

She felt as if she had stumbled into a strange world.

Everything was different from anything that she had ever seen before.

She was so intent on what she was seeing that she was not looking ahead and suddenly she realised that she had almost fallen over a man who was sitting on a low stool.

In front of him was an easel on which stood a canvas.

He was obviously painting the lake and concentrating intently on his work so that he was not aware of her presence.

She glanced at his canvas and thought that as a painter he was obviously very talented and she noted to herself that he was the first person she had seen since leaving The Palace so early this morning

She hoped that he might be able to tell her what she wished to know.

"Excuse me, *mein herr*," she began politely, "can you tell me where – ?"

Before she could finish the sentence, the artist exclaimed,

"Go away! Leave me alone! I am busy!"

He spoke so angrily that Thea was astonished.

Apart from her father nobody had ever spoken to her in such a way.

For a moment she did not move and then, as if he was intending to order her to obey him, the artist turned his head.

He looked at Thea and was then astonished into silence.

He just sat on his wooden staring at her.

She was looking at him as well, finding it strange that anyone so rude could be so good-looking. He was unlike any man she had ever seen before.

He had dark hair, which was uncovered, straight classical features and what she thought were almost black eyes.

There seemed to be a long silence before he began,

"I do apologise. I was not expecting to be visited by a Goddess from the heart of one of the mountains!"

Because she could not help it, Thea laughed.

She had always believed that there were Gods and Goddesses living on top of the snow-capped mountains.

They would show their disapproval of anyone by sending down cascades of icy water or would reward those they favoured with an abundance of delicious wild strawberries.

As he went on gazing at Thea, the artist rose to his feet.

He was tall, over six foot and his shoulders were broad and she realised that he showed his profession by the way he was dressed.

He had discarded his coat because the sun was warm, especially as the lake was sheltered by so many trees.

He was wearing instead of a tie, a red silk scarf round his neck that was tied in a large bow.

As Thea did not speak, the artist then said,

"Please forgive me and let me try to answer the question you were asking me that I did not allow you to finish."

He seemed so contrite that Thea smiled and replied,

"Maybe it is I who should apologise for interrupting you when you are painting anything so beautiful."

"I was cross because I could not capture it," the artist admitted. "How can I depict the dancing lights on the water and the mystery of the trees?"

Thea stared at him in astonishment.

It was exactly what she thought herself, but nobody else had ever said it to her before.

"May I look at your painting?" she asked him.

The artist spread out his hands.

"I am honoured that you should do so. At the same time I am well aware that I am an inadequate painter."

Thea moved closer to his easel.

She could see at first glance that the painting was very different from any of the pictures hanging on the walls of The Palace.

It was not in any way a precise representation of the lake or the trees.

It was, she thought, more of an impression and yet in some strange way he had captured the magic of the lake and its surrounds that more traditional artists would not have been able to achieve.

She was gazing intently at it unaware that the artist was watching her.

At length she declared,

"I think you are painting what you feel rather than what you see. It is very clever. I can feel the goblins under the trees and the nymphs beneath the water!"

She was speaking to herself rather than to him, then, as he did not reply, she turned to look at him.

"You *are* a Goddess from the mountains!" he exclaimed. "And no one else has ever understood what I am trying to do."

'It is – difficult to put into – words."

"Of course," he answered, "but what you are thinking and feeling is very much more important."

Thea was going to ask him how he could speak like that when Mercury came to join her.

At the sound of the horse the artist turned his head to look with even more amazement at the huge black stallion with just a white star on his forehead.

"So this is how you reached me!" he cried.

"This is Mercury," Thea said by way of introduction.

"The Messenger of the Gods!" the artist exclaimed. "How could he be anything else?"

He patted Mercury on the neck and he nuzzled Thea affectionately and then she said,

"What I was going to ask you was if you knew of anywhere near here where Mercury and I could have – something to eat. We have – travelled a – long way this morning."

"I can understand that," the artist said, glancing up at the mountain peaks directly above them, "but I am afraid I cannot offer you ambrosia!"

"I will accept – anything that is – edible," Thea smiled.

As she thought about it, she was indeed feeling hungry, having eaten nothing since last night.

Even then because her father had upset her, she had only picked at the food that Martha had brought to her bedroom.

She had been thinking all the time of having to marry the old King Otho and the food had therefore seemed to stick in her throat.

The artist closed his paintbox and put his canvas under his arm.

He left both the easel and the stool where they were, making it clear that he intended to come back later for them.

Thea thought that he was not taking the risk of losing his picture although she doubted if there was anybody in the vicinity who was likely to steal it.

Then, as an afterthought, he asked her,

"Do you wish to ride or will you walk? It is not very far."

"I will walk," Thea answered.

They moved along a track that wound through the wood and Mercury followed behind them like a faithful dog would do.

"I feel rather guilty," Thea said conversationally, "for taking you away from your work. You could have told me where I could go."

"Apart from the fact that it would be impolite," the artist replied, "I have just realised that I am hungry."

Thea laughed.

"I feel the same, but I was so enjoying my ride that I forgot everything else."

"Are you really riding alone?" the artist enquired.

"Yes."

The one syllable told him better than more words that she did not wish to speak about it.

He glanced at her profile because she was now looking away from him and there was a twinkle in his eyes, but he did not say anything more.

They walked in silence until the trees suddenly came to an end and there, just in front of them, was a small building.

It was perched on the side of a mountain with a cliff below it that fell hundreds of feet down into a valley.

Thea looked down in surprise.

It was a very different valley from the one that she had just left. To begin with there were many more woods and it all seemed to be wild and uncultivated, but at the same time very beautiful.

There were no mountains straight ahead of them and the land seemed to just go on into infinity.

She realised suddenly that this was another country and that she had left her own.

But for the moment she did not want to ask the artist any questions.

She was so afraid that she would find that she was in Kanaris and that was King Otho's Kingdom.

The artist was now leading her towards the small house.

As they drew nearer to it, Thea thought that it was a very strange place to find a hotel.

As far as she could see, either beyond or below it, there was no other building.

She was just about to ask the artist for an explanation when a young man came hurrying towards him.

"I just coming, Master," he said, "to tell you time for luncheon."

"Tell your mother I have a guest for luncheon," the artist ordered, "and tell Valou that there is a hungry horse that requires a stable."

The boy looked at Mercury and then he ran to do the artist's bidding.

Thea was at once aware that both the artist and the boy had spoken in a language that was different from the language of Kostas.

She could fully understand what he was saying and she knew that she had learnt their language, but for the moment she could not put a name to it.

They had gone on for a short distance before an older man appeared and Thea thought that he would be recognisable anywhere as being connected with horses.

He gave an exclamation when he saw Mercury and it was one of admiration.

"Give him a good meal, Valou," the artist said, "which is what I intend to have myself."

The groom bowed politely to Thea as he passed her and then he patted Mercury before he took him by the bridle.

When the horse went with him without making a fuss, Thea knew immediately that he was experienced with animals.

"We go this way," the artist suggested.

She saw that he was taking her to the front of the small house.

There was a balcony outside and she could see that there was a table already laid for one with a white tablecloth. It had an orange-coloured umbrella above it to keep off the sun.

The artist, however, walked in through the door that led into the hall. Thea, following him, found that it was very different from what she had expected.

The hall was small and painted white. The only decoration consisted of several paintings like the one that the artist had been working on by the lake.

At a glance she could see that all the paintings had the same characteristics that made her appreciate that he was painting what he felt.

"If you go up the stairs," he said, "you will find a room on the left where I am sure you would like to wash your hands."

"Thank you," Thea replied.

She went up the stairs thinking that this was indeed an unexpected adventure.

She found the room, which was not difficult, as there were only two doors at the top of the stairs, one to the right and one to the left.

The room that she had been directed to was as surprising as the hall. It was small, but the window had a glorious view over the valley below that was breathtaking.

Most of the room seemed to be filled with a very large bed that was distinctive because the back, the sides and the feet were all carved and painted.

Thea knew that it was the work of local craftsmen, but the workmanship was far superior to anything that she had seen before.

The headboard depicted flowers that she had seen by the lake, a great number of which she reckoned were wild. And amongst them nestled birds and most of them she knew by name.

There were one or two, however, that were strangers to Thea.

Their brilliant plumage, the colours of the flowers and the skilful manner that they had been massed together was lovely.

For a moment she could only stand staring at it and then she realised that the bed cover was also the product of local talent.

There were many women in Kostas who made lace with their bobbins and what she was looking at now was outstanding work and very lovely indeed.

On the polished wooden floor there were white rugs of chamois skin.

She washed her hands in a china bowl which she was quite certain was the work of local potters.

It was all so fascinating and intriguing.

She admired it for some time before she looked for a mirror, which again was carved very delicately and was surmounted by two fat little cupids who had been coloured in natural hues.

She next tidied her hair, which had been swept into curls by the wild way that she had galloped on Mercury.

Then she went down the stairs.

The artist was waiting for her on the balcony outside. She was sure it was a concession that he had put on a coat of some light material and a different scarf at his neck and this time it was blue and it too was tied in a bow in the front.

She wondered if he wore the velvet tam-o'-shanter that was usually adopted by French artists.

She had, however, no wish to ask him any uncomfortable questions or to appear critical in any way.

She saw, as she joined her host, that another chair had been placed beside the table.

She sat down under the shade of the orange umbrella, the sun was high in the sky and it was becoming increasingly hot.

As if he read her thoughts, the artist suggested,

"Why do you not take off your riding coat?"

"What a good idea," Thea nodded.

He helped her out of her coat and, as he put it down on a chair, she looked at the view and said,

"I think I am dreaming! I had no idea that anything could be quite so glorious."

"Nor had I," the artist replied, but he was looking at her.

He poured something from a jug into her glass and, when she looked at it, he explained,

"It is a fruit juice that is a local speciality. I do hope you will enjoy it."

She lifted it to her lips and found it delicious and then, because she was curious, she had to ask him,

"Is this your house? Do you live here?"

"It is my house," he replied.

"How could you have found anything so different – so unusual?" Thea asked.

"I must have known instinctively that one day it would be what you wanted," he replied.

She laughed.

"That is a pretty speech, but I think that it was very clever of you to discover anything so unique!"

"I thought so myself."

Once again he was gazing at her.

It flashed through her mind how shocked her father and mother would be that she was alone with a very handsome young man in a house where there was no chaperone.

The boy who had met them at the lake brought out the first dish.

Now, as he came towards the table, he was not in his shirtsleeves. He had put on a clean white jacket and he had brushed his hair.

"I usually have a small luncheon," the artist was saying, "but I promise to provide you with something more exotic at dinner."

Thea's eyes opened wide.

"Dinner?" she exclaimed. "But I was – not planning to – stay."

"Where are you going?"

She realised that she had no answer to this question and after a moment she said,

"I-I am not quite – certain but – further on."

"Why?"

There really seemed to be no answer to that.

She had to be as far as possible from The Palace, but it was something that she could not say to her charming host.

They were eating a salad of eggs, fish, lettuce and tomatoes.

Because she was hungry, Thea thought that every mouthful was a real joy.

It was followed promptly by a dish of young tender chicken cooked with cream and it was flavoured with some herbs that Thea did not recognise.

There were tiny potatoes, so small that it seemed cruel to eat them, peas that were also minute and little carrots no bigger than Thea's smallest finger.

After this there was cheese of several different varieties.

Coffee, black and fragrant, completed one of the most delicious meals that Thea had ever enjoyed.

They did not talk much while they were eating and, when they had finished, the artist sat back in his chair.

"Now tell me about yourself," he proposed. "First of all I don't know your name."

"It is 'Thea'."

She knew as she spoke that she was quite safe in saying that for only her family called her 'Thea' and to the people of Kostas she was 'Princess Sydel'.

"But I don't know your name," she said, "and I just cannot go on thinking of you as 'the artist'."

He laughed.

"That is a compliment, but I am too conscious of my obvious shortcomings to be entitled to it."

"Of course you are entitled to it," Thea argued. "It is only that I have the idea that you are in advance of our time. One day people will understand what you are trying to say in your paintings."

"How do you know that?" he enquired.

Thea made a little gesture that explained better than words it was just what she thought.

"Who are you?" he asked. "And where are you going all alone with a horse that could only have come from Mount Olympus."

Thea did not answer and after a moment he asked her,

"I know without you telling me that you are running away."

She looked at him with startled eyes.

"Why – should you – think that?"

"Why should you understand what I am trying to paint?" he retorted.

She decided that there was no point in prevaricating any further.

"Yes – I am running – away."

"From a man?"

"Y-yes – a man!"

That was certainly true and, as she thought of King Otho, she shuddered.

"Then I can think of no place where you are less likely to be disturbed than here," the artist responded.

"No – no – of course – not!" Thea replied.

"Why not?"

"Because you are a stranger and – I don't – know you!"

"My name is 'Nikōs' and I think that we know each other very much better than if we had been introduced formally at a Reception, which would have been incredibly dull except that you were there!"

Because of the way he spoke Thea could not help laughing.

Nikōs bent towards her.

"Why are you running away?"

"Because – I want to be – free!"

"That is a cry from all down the ages, but unfortunately it is impossible."

"Why is it – impossible?"

"Because you are a woman and women have to be protected, cared for and looked after."

"That is something I have – no wish to be. I want to be – myself. I want to – live my own life."

"And to find what you are seeking?" Nikōs said gently.

For a moment she was startled.

Then she told herself that he was being uncannily perceptive, but he could not know that what she was really seeking was *love*.

The love that she was cruelly denied because she was a Princess.

CHAPTER THREE

When luncheon was over, Nikōs turned to Thea,

"There are places in the wood that I would very much like to show you. Another day I will take you riding."

Thea looked at him with wide eyes and he added,

"Both you and Mercury have gone far enough today. It would really be cruelty to take your plucky stallion any further."

She opened her lips to say that she could not stay with him as he had suggested.

And then she asked herself 'why not?'

She had to stay somewhere for the night and it suddenly struck her that if she was in a hotel she might well be frightened and intimidated.

She had not thought of this before, but, of course, there might be strange men.

Although Nikōs was what the English would undoubtedly call 'a gentleman', other men might be rough and threatening and try to take advantage of her.

They also might be overfamiliar, she thought, which was something that she had never encountered in her whole sheltered life.

She therefore did not answer him directly and, as if he took it for granted that she would do as he suggested, they went into the woods.

Everything in the woods like the thick fir trees and the glimmering forest pools seemed even more enchanted as if from another world.

She was vividly conscious of the mountain peaks high overhead and wherever there was a clearing in the trees she could look at the overwhelmingly beautiful views, which seemed to change so rapidly with the clouds scuddering across the wild sky.

It was the beautiful valley that she had seen from Nikōs's house.

They did not talk much at first and yet strangely enough Thea felt as if he understood what she was thinking.

She thought too that she could read his thoughts very clearly.

Finally they sat down on a mossy bank that sloped down to a small pool in which the water lilies had first come into flower.

"It is so unbelievably – lovely that I am sure that I must be dreaming," Thea sighed.

"That is what I have felt ever since I saw you!" Nikōs said.

She felt the colour rise in her cheeks, but she did not look at him and after a moment he said,

"I had forgotten that a woman could blush or that she could look shy!"

"You must – not say – such things to me," Thea said in a low voice.

"Why not? I want to tell you how beautiful you are, how intelligent and – "

He hesitated.

Because she was feeling curious, she could not resist glancing at him, hoping that he would finish the sentence.

Unexpectedly he said abruptly,

"We should be getting back to the house. The sun is not as warm as it was."

He spoke in a distant voice about a marsh, which made Thea feel as if she had suddenly been touched by a cold hand.

Nikōs had now risen to his feet.

He was walking slowly back along the twisting path that they had followed through the trees.

Suddenly Thea felt frightened, she did not understand what was happening to her now and why Nikōs had so suddenly changed his attitude towards her.

She stood up and ran after him and. as she reached his side, she asked,

"What – is the – matter? What – have I done wrong?"

For a moment she thought that he would not reply to her.

Then he said,

"The only thing that is wrong is that you are too beautiful for any man's peace of mind!"

"I-I cannot help – my looks."

"What you *can* help," he replied almost angrily, "is wandering about the country on your own. It is something seriously foolhardy that you should never do again."

She did not answer and he went on almost as if he was speaking to himself.

"I should send you back, otherwise you will get into endless trouble."

"S-send me – back? No – *no*! I will – not go!"

Now there was a note of fear in her voice.

"It is something that I ought to do," he pronounced.

"But – why? You have – no right. It is – not your – business."

He stopped and turned to face her.

"If I leave you to go your own way, what will happen to you?"

"I was – thinking about – that and – perhaps it would be – very frightening."

He did not say anything and she then looked up at him.

"Please – let me – stay with you," she asked him pleadingly.

"Is that what you want?"

"I was – thinking that it could be – very difficult for me to stay in a – hotel."

"Very difficult indeed," he nodded.

"I-I did not – think of that when I – ran away."

She saw by the expression on his face what Nikōs was thinking.

"Let me stay – please – let me stay," she asked again, "at least for – tonight."

He smiled.

"As you have come many miles, I really have no choice."

"I will be no – trouble, I promise – and if you want – I will leave here early in the – morning."

"We will discuss that when the morning comes."

She now knew that she could stay and she felt a sudden overwhelming relief.

"Thank you," she sighed. "Thank you – very much!"

"I think I must add a condition to my invitation," Nikōs said.

"What is – it?" Thea enquired nervously.

"That you tell me why you have run away and from whom!"

She stiffened.

"I-I don't want – to tell anyone and it is a – secret!"

She sounded agitated, so he capitulated.

"Very well, keep your secrets and, as you told me that you want to be free, let's just enjoy ourselves."

Thea's eyes lit up.

"That would be – lovely! And when we – go back to the – house I would like to see – Mercury."

"Of course!" Nikōs agreed. "But I can assure you that he is very comfortable. Valou will see to that."

They walked on a little way along the path.

Then Nikōs wanted to know,

"How can you have acquired such a remarkably outstanding horse?"

"I have had him since he was a foal and I love him more than anyone else – in the whole world!"

Nikōs raised his eyebrows.

"That is very sweeping."

"It is true. I am happiest when I am with Mercury and he understands everything when I talk to him like – "

She stopped feeling that what she had been about to say was too intimate.

" – like I do!" Nikōs said softly.

"I-I did not say – that."

"But it is what you were thinking."

"Now you are – reading my – thoughts and it is – something you must not do."

"It is too late for you to stop me doing something that has happened amazingly since you first appeared here."

Thea walked on a little way before she commented,

"It is very strange – but no one before has ever – understood what I was thinking – and what I – try to express in my music."

"I might have guessed you were musical," Nikōs remarked.

"Why?"

"Because everything about you is an entrancing poem, your looks, the way you walk and your voice."

Thea looked at him with her green eyes.

"That is a lovely thing to tell me and something that I will always remember."

"I have always been told that the women of Kostas have musical voices," Nikōs said, "but yours is like the song of the birds."

Thea made a little murmur and he went on,

"I know without you telling me that there is Hungarian blood in your veins."

"My grandmother was Hungarian."

"And so was mine!" Nikōs exclaimed. "That is another bond we have in common."

Thea laughed.

"And I am sure you ride like a Hungarian."

"As you do."

The little house was in sight and now the sun was sinking low over the plain. It turned everything to gold and made the world so extraordinarily beautiful that Thea drew in her breath.

"Shall I try to paint it for you?" Nikōs suggested softly.

"That is what I would really – like you to do."

Then with a little start she said,

"You are reading my – thoughts again!"

"Your eyes are very revealing, but I feel that it would be impossible to depict them on canvas."

"I am glad about that. I hate being painted."

She thought of the long sittings that she had had to endure because some organisations in Gyula were always asking for a portrait of her. She was hung in schools and in the Council Chamber and she thought how different those portraits were from the paintings completed by Nikōs.

Sitting stiffly in white satin with a pink curtain draped behind her with her hands in her lap and she looked very unlike herself.

"I will paint you against the trees with your face reflected in the lake where we met," Nikōs suggested.

Thea smiled, but, before she could say that it was what she would like, he went on,

"I will show you as you are, ethereal, half-human and half a 'spirit of the woods'."

He spoke in a low voice and then as if with effort, he said,

"It will soon be time for dinner and Valou's wife will be arranging a bath for you in your bedroom."

"That will be lovely!" Thea exclaimed.

She smiled at him and walked up the stairs.

As he had told her, there was a bath arranged in the same way as she always had it at The Palace.

There was a large can of hot water and another smaller one of cold and the bath was already half-full.

The water in the bath was scented with the fragrance of jasmine and there were several half-open blossoms floating in it.

As she bathed in the delicious warm water, she thought that this was the most exciting adventure she could imagine.

'How could I have been so lucky, so incredibly fortunate as to find anyone as interesting as Nikōs?' she asked herself.

She thought of the dull and dreary conversations she had with the Courtiers in the Palace and the way that Nikōs had talked this afternoon was like the music she played on the piano.

Being with Georgi was always fun, but he was not interested in anything she thought or said, he only wanted her to listen to him.

He would now be happy enjoying himself in Paris, she reflected.

She wished that she could see the women who amused him and the theatres and dances he would be attending.

Georgi had told her that her mother and father would be shocked at everything he did and it was difficult for Thea to imagine exactly why.

'Georgi is enjoying himself and so am I!' she ruminated to herself defiantly.

By now they would be aware at The Palace that she was missing, but she was sure that her father would not wish to publicise the matter in case her disappearance became a scandal and he would he want many people to find out that she had flown the nest.

She thought it over carefully and she expected that he would first of all send *aides-de-camp* to all the places where she was likely to be.

She had an old Governess who had retired to live in a small village about four miles from Gyula. They would go to her and, of course, they would call on the Professor.

She thought of the other Teachers she had had in the past and knew that it would take time to visit them all.

After that King Otho would arrive and her father would have to make some excuse for her not being present.

He might say that she was ill or staying with some elderly relatives. He could hardly tell King Otho that she had run away because she did not want to marry him.

As always, when she was thinking of King Otho, she shuddered.

'When he has gone home to his own country,' she told herself, 'I suppose I shall have to go back to The Palace.'

Then she thought that she was in no hurry as yet, but sooner or later she would have to return.

As she stepped out of the bath, she escaped from reality and as always she slipped into one of her many Fairy stories.

Perhaps she could find a little house like this for herself and live quietly in the country with Mercury.

She would make friends with the peasants and with the gypsies for there were certain to be some camping in the neighbourhood.

She would need money. She would ask the women who had made the lace cover on her bed to teach her how to do it.

It was a simple tale of contentment and once again, as if he was an evil genie threatening her, she could see King Otho.

He would be waiting for her and, when she was back at The Palace, it would only be a question of whether he came to her or she went to him.

Her father would by now have pledged his word to King Otho that she would be his wife.

Because she was so terrified by the idea, Thea dressed hurriedly.

She wanted to go back to Nikōs and she would talk to him about the woods, the birds and the flowers as well as the Fairies, elves and water nymphs that they both believed in.

She put on her muslin gown. It was a very simple one, made with the material drawn back into classical folds in the front.

The only concession to the fashionable bustle was a sash of the same material. It had silver threads running through it and ended in a huge bow at the back.

There were frills round the low neck and small puffed sleeves and it made her look very young and at the same time there was something very Grecian about her.

When she came down the stairs, Nikōs was waiting for her at the bottom step.

As she reached him, he said,

"Now I know that you have come from the mountain peaks and you are in fact Divine!"

Thea smiled.

"After that pretty speech, it may sound very mundane for me to tell you that I am very hungry."

He laughed and it was a very happy sound.

"No one but you, Thea," he replied, "would say that at this particular moment."

She did not understand what he meant.

He took her into a room that she had not seen before because for luncheon they had sat out on the terrace.

It was a very attractive room with a huge window overlooking the valley and it had a large fireplace in which there was a big log burning.

She was not surprised, because now that the sun had gone down, it could be very cold with icy winds blowing down from the snow-capped peaks.

The room was warm and, although it was white, like the rest of the house, it was also very masculine.

The sofa and chairs were large and comfortable and the floor was covered with fur rugs.

Besides the pictures that had been painted by Nikōs, there was a sporting gun and two rifles hanging on the wall.

A magnificent stag's head with long horns towered over the fireplace.

Thea looked up at it and said,

"Somehow I cannot imagine you — shooting in the woods."

"You are quite right. It is something I don't do!"

She looked at he stag's head without asking the obvious question.

"It was given to me by one of the woodcutters when I first came here," Nikōs explained. "It was his finest possession and he told me that it would bring me luck."

"And has it?"

"What could be luckier than that I should find you?"

Thea smiled.

She had no idea that Nikōs was thinking that she was very unlike any other woman he had known before in his life.

There was nothing in the least flirtatious in the way she looked at him when he paid her a compliment.

"And the gun?" she questioned.

"It was given to me by a gypsy I befriended when I first came here."

He had also been given the rifles. They were elaborately decorated in the style of the beginning of the century.

The gun was old as well and its butt was carved with miniature animals, each one more exquisite and more lifelike than the last.

"Dinner is served, Master."

It was the boy who had waited on them at luncheon, who spoke from the doorway.

"Thank you, Géza," Nikōs said.

He held out his arm with a mocking smile to Thea and, as she took it, she noticed for the first time how he was dressed.

It was in an even more picturesque way than he had been dressed in the daytime.

He wore a white shirt and over it a black velvet coat, which she might have expected on an artist. Round his waist was a red cummerbund and the silk scarf round his neck was equally attractive.

On any other man it might have looked rather affected, but on Nikōs it only added, Thea mused, to his aura of masculinity.

She had been conscious of it ever since they first met.

Now he took her into the dining room, which was another room that she had not seen before. It was smaller and the curtains were drawn over the windows, which looked out onto the woods.

They were unlike any curtains that she had ever seen.

Only as she looked a little closer at them did she realise that Nikōs had painted them.

There was an impression of the snow-capped mountains and also the flowers that she had seen this afternoon, irises and water lilies, white and blue violets and wild orchids.

It was quite lovely.

As she was trying to think of the right words to tell Nikōs just how clever she thought he was, he said,

"I knew you would appreciate them."

There was a round table in the centre of the room and it was covered with a lace cloth rather like the cover of her bed.

The tall candelabrum in the middle of it, which held six candles, was of pottery and again Thea was certain that it was made by talented local craftsmen.

It showed the stems of flowers entwined together to make the shaft of the candelabrum and the candles sat in the open petals of the flowers.

Géza brought in the food, which was as unusual as it was delicious.

There were small river crabs cooked in a way that Thea had never met before.

There were partridges prepared in red wine that seemed to melt in the mouth and cutlets of tiny baby lamb.

To finish they had small strawberries that must have just ripened in the sun.

Nikōs insisted that she should drink the 'wine of the country'.

As she sipped it, Thea realised that she still did not know and she was too afraid to ask if she was in King Otho's Kingdom.

When they had finished the superb dinner, she said,

"I have never, and this is the truth, had a more delicious dinner."

"That is what I want you to say," Nikōs smiled, "and Valou's wife will be delighted at your praise."

"If you eat like this every day," Thea pointed out, "I cannot imagine how you remain so slim!"

She had realised when they were walking together in the wood that there was something very athletic in the way he moved.

"Tomorrow," he said quietly, "when we ride together, you will realise that there is no better exercise."

"That is what I have always believed. I want to ride and ride every day so that I shall never grow fat."

Nikōs laughed.

"I am sure that is an impossibility and I am only afraid that you will fly away from me on the wind.'

They went back into the sitting room.

Now the flames were high over the log in the fireplace, the curtains had been drawn and it was warm and very cosy.

Thea sat down, not in a chair, but on the fur rug in front of the fire.

The light on her hair seemed to echo the flames and Nikōs was sitting gazing at her.

Then, as the warmth made her yawn, he commented,

"You are tired."

"I was up very early," she answered.

"How early?"

"Dawn had not yet broken."

"Then you must go to bed at once."

She did not reply and after a moment he asked her,

"Have you enjoyed your first day of freedom?"

"It has been wonderful! More exciting than I can possibly say."

"What will you do when you have to go back?"

"I have decided I will not go back!"

"Never?"

"Never!" Thea averred firmly.

She thought if she did, however long she had stayed away, she would still be forced to marry King Otho.

She would find some place where her father would never discover her and she would have Mercury with her – so that nothing else in the world mattered.

Nikōs did not speak, he was only watching her closely.

Because Thea thought that he wanted to retire, she rose to her feet.

"You are right," she sighed, "I will go to bed. There is always tomorrow and thank you for being so kind to me."

He had risen as she had and now he stood with his back to the fire looking at her.

"As you say," he said in a deep voice, "there is always tomorrow and indeed the day after."

She smiled and he went on,

"What matters is that we have found each other!"

As he spoke, he put his arms round her and drew her against him.

It was so unexpected that Thea hardly realised what was happening.

Then his lips were on hers.

She was so surprised that she did not struggle.

She only knew that she had not realised that a kiss could hold her completely captive so that she felt that it was impossible to move.

Then she felt a very strange sensation she had never known before streaking through her body.

It was like the first notes of a sonata.

Only this was music that was playing in her heart.

She felt Nikōs's arms tighten round her

His lips became more insistent, demanding and possessive.

She was not frightened.

It was the magic of the fir trees, the enchantment of the flowers and the shimmering light on the water.

He kissed her until she felt that her whole body was pulsating with magic.

She had always known that it was there inside her if she could but find it.

Only when he raised his head did she stare at him, her breath was coming quickly from between her parted lips.

"Go to bed, my lovely," he said in a voice that was very deep and a little hoarse.

It was impossible to speak, because he had carried her up to the mountain peaks.

Thea obeyed him and, moving swiftly across the room without looking back, she opened the door.

She ran up the stairs into her bedroom.

There was only one candle burning by the side of the bed and her nightgown had been laid out for her.

The flowers on the headboard seemed a part of the dream world that Nikōs had taken her into.

She undressed quickly and climbed into bed.

Only when she was lying back against the pillows could she think and ask herself how it was possible to feel such rapture.

It was different from anything that she had ever felt before.

Yet it was familiar because she had known that it was there.

She had known it when she played the piano and known it when she heard the song of the birds.

She had known it when she looked out over the valley and when she felt the beauty of it tug at her heart.

She felt as if she was still being carried towards the mountain peaks and to the stars that were shining so brightly overhead.

The magic in the woods was whispering a song that she could only sing in her heart.

She was just about to blow out the candle by the bed.

Then to her surprise the door opened and Nikōs came in.

He had undressed and was wearing a long robe that was crimson and frogged with gold braid.

He looked different, somehow larger and yet even more attractive.

He came towards the bed and, as Thea looked at him with wide eyes, he sat down on it facing her.

With difficulty, because she had to come back from her dreams, she found her voice.

"W-what do you – want? Why – are you – h-here?"

"I did not finish saying 'goodnight' to you."

"B-but – I do *not* – think you should – come to my room."

"Why not?"

"It is – incorrect."

"What we have already done can hardly be called correct," Nikōs parried. "And I think, my darling, you want me a little as I want you overwhelmingly!"

"I-I don't – understand."

"Then let me make it clearer. I will look after you, protect you and hide you if that is what you want."

"I want that – but I still do not – think we need talk about – it when I am in bed."

He looked at her piercingly until, as he realised that she really did not understand, he said,

"What I am trying to say, perhaps inadequately, is that I will teach you about love. You will feel even more ecstatic than you felt just now when I kissed you."

"It was – wonderful!" Thea admitted, "but I think – " She stopped and gave a little cry, "Are you saying that you – want to – make love to me?"

"Yes, that is what I want."

"But – of course you must not do that!"

"Why not?"

"Because – it is wrong – very wrong."

"Why should you think that? How could anything so wonderful be wrong?"

He did not wait for Thea to reply, but bent forward towards her.

For a moment her lips were very soft beneath his.

Then, as she excited him so that he could no longer go on talking, he put his arms around her.

At the same time he lifted his feet onto the bed.

His lips became fiercer and Thea felt again the wonder that he had given her when he had first kissed her.

Then she was aware that his hand was touching her breast and she struggled.

"I want you – God how I want you!" Nikōs asserted.

"Please – you must not – do this!" she gasped.

She did not think that he could have heard her for now he was kissing her neck.

She felt a thrill that was like a streak of forked lightning running through her body.

Then he was pushing the sheet lower and his hand was moving down her body.

She pressed her hands against his chest and then realised how strong he was.

Now she was frightened – really frightened.

"Stop! Please – *stop*!" she pleaded.

It was as if Nikōs did not hear.

"I am – frightened! You are – frightening – me. Please – *please* – Nikōs – listen to me! I am – frightened."

It was the cry of a child.

And it stopped him in a way that nothing else would have done.

He raised his head as if he could not believe what he had heard.

He looked down at her.

He saw the terror in her eyes and the tears that were now running down her cheeks.

"I am – so frightened!" she repeated. "I-I don't know – what you are – doing, but I – know it is – wrong!"

The words fell over themselves and her tears blinded her eyes.

He gazed at her for one long moment and then very slowly he moved off the bed to sit facing her as he had done before.

It was impossible for Thea to stop crying.

But the light from the candle turned her hair to flaming gold and her skin was very white and translucent.

She had no idea how utterly desirable she looked.

"Please – please," she said again incoherently.

Taking a handkerchief from the pocket of his robe, Nikōs bent forward and wiped the tears from her eyes.

"It's all right," he reassured her. "I will not hurt you."

Now he could see that the pupils of her eyes were dilated and she was trembling.

"I will not hurt you," he said again. "At the same time I don't understand."

"You are – not angry?"

"Only bewildered," he replied. "How can you wander about the countryside alone, talk to a strange man and stay in his house?"

"You – asked me to – stay!"

He smiled.

"Yes, I asked you and it seemed the obvious thing to do."

He paused before he went on,

"Have you no idea of the dangers you might encounter, in fact have encountered?"

"I-I did not – think of – it," Thea said hesitatingly.

"You make it very difficult for me or any other man."

"Why?"

"You know the answer to that! You are very beautiful and very desirable."

She looked at him as if she was puzzling out what he meant.

Then she asked.

"Do you mean – because I look – pretty it makes – you want to do – what is wrong?"

"It depends what you mean by wrong. I want to make love to you and I want to make you mine."

She looked at him and she was still trembling.

"But I promise you that I will not do anything that makes you so frightened," he said quietly, "although it is going to be hard if you stay with me."

"Do you want me to – go away?"

The fear was back in Thea's voice and Nikōs smiled.

"No, I want you to stay, you know that."

She looked at him uncertainly.

"Perhaps – I should – go."

It flashed through her mind that if she did there were bound to be other men.

They would come to her room as Nikōs had done. They might try to make love to her whether she tried to stop them or not.

As if he knew what she was thinking, he said,

"You can stay here, at least for a little while, but it would be much easier if you did what I wanted."

He thought that the fear was back in her eyes and he suggested gently,

"We will talk about it tomorrow. Go to sleep now and don't be afraid. The dragons are all gone!"

"You – promise you – are not – angry with me?"

There was a little twist to his lips as Nikōs replied,

"Shall I say I am disappointed?"

He took her hand and raised it to her lips.

"Goodnight, Ice Maiden, and another time remember to lock your door."

He pulled himself off the bed as he spoke.

"Do you mean – " Thea asked, "so that you should not – come in?"

He did not reply and she said almost beneath her breath,

"I never – thought of it."

Nikōs had reached the door.

"Forget it and go to sleep," he said. "As you said earlier, there is always tomorrow."

"And – you will be – here?"

"I promise you I will not disappear in the night, but you must promise me the same."

Then he went out and closed the door quietly behind him.

She heard him cross the landing and go into the room opposite.

Then there was silence.

She did not blow out the candle at first and instead she lay in bed thinking of what had just happened.

Insidiously the rapture that she had felt when Nikōs kissed her came back and she felt the wonder of it within her breast.

She could feel too the lightning that had swept through her when he had kissed her neck.

To her horror she then found herself wondering why she had stopped him.

Why had she not let him make love to her as he had wanted to?

'It is wrong – *wicked* – and, if I had done so – I would be like the – women who Georgi enjoys himself with – when he is in Paris.'

Yet she wanted Nikōs to kiss her again and she wanted him to touch her.

How was it possible that she should feel like this for a man she had never seen until this morning?

Yet he had always been in her dreams and in the stories she told herself.

He was the Prince Charming who would appear unexpectedly and he would love her as she would love him.

Then she knew that in the Fairytale the Prince asked her to be his wife.

When she said 'yes', they were married and lived happily ever after.

Innocent though she was, Thea knew only too well that Nikōs did not wish to marry her.

He wanted to be her lover.

'It would be wrong – very wrong – for me to – agree to anything that was – so wicked,' she told herself.

But her lips were aching for his kisses and now he had gone she wanted him to stay.

It flashed through her mind that she had only to cross from her room to his and they would be together.

She was shocked at her own feelings and her own thoughts.

She knew then instinctively that she could not possibly stay.

She jumped up, took off her nightgown and dressed herself in her riding habit.

It was hanging in the wardrobe and so were the few other things that she had brought with her. She put them in the woollen shawl that had been attached to her saddle and then she wrapped her slippers and her hairbrush in her blue chiffon scarf.

When she was ready, she peeped through the curtains.

To her relief she saw that there was a moon that was turning everything outside to silver and it would make it easier for her to find her way to the stables.

She would collect Mercury and ride away.

Very very softly, she opened the door of her bedroom and on tiptoe she went down the stairs.

Everything was silent.

She thought that, if one of the wooden stairs creaked, it would be like a pistol shot.

There was moonlight coming from two glass windows on either side of the door.

As she reached it, she saw that there were two bolts, one up high and the other low down.

She had to balance on tiptoe to reach the higher bolt.

She was just drawing it back, finding it rather stiff, when a voice behind her asked,

"Where do you think you are going?"

She started and turned round.

In the moonlight she could see Nikōs standing at the top of the stairs.

He was wearing the crimson robe that he had worn when he came to her room.

He walked down the stairs towards her.

She felt that he was very large and overpowering, while she was like a schoolgirl who had been caught out playing truant.

He came nearer.

Just as he reached the last step, she turned round to stand at the window with her back to him.

She thought that he was going to be angry with her and she was trembling.

'I have – to go! I – have to go – away,' she told herself.

Then Nikōs was just behind her and to her surprise his voice was quiet and gentle as he asked,

"Why are you leaving me?"

"I-I have – to!"

"Why?"

She tried to find the words and, because she did not speak, Nikōs asked again,

"Why are you going?"

Thea then told him the truth.

"Because – I want to – stay with you."

For a moment there was silence before he replied,

"My darling, I was a fool to frighten you."

He drew in his breath and then, almost as if he was speaking to himself, he said,

"I had no idea that you were so young, so innocent and so unspoilt."

"I-I have to – go," Thea persisted. "I will – find somewhere – else to stay."

"You really think that I would let you do anything quite so dangerous?" Nikōs asked. "Or so incredibly foolish?"

Because his voice was so kind and because she was still frightened, once again Thea was crying.

Nikōs did not say anything more, he merely bent down and picked her up in his arms.

Clutching her two bundles against her breast, Thea put her head against his shoulder and closed her eyes.

She was aware of the security of his arms and the comfort of being so close to him.

The world outside was dark and she was sure that there were dragons waiting to attack her.

Nikōs carried her up the stairs and back into her bedroom.

He set her gently down on the bed and, taking her bundles from her, he put them on a chair.

Then he suggested,

"I want you to go to sleep. Tomorrow we will make plans, but now you are very tired."

"I-I thought – you would be – asleep," Thea stammered.

"I was sitting thinking about you."

"As I – thought about – you."

"I think, my darling," he said, "you were loving me, as I was loving you."

Thea looked at him with wide eyes.

"How – how do you – know that?"

He smiled.

"We know so much about each other, how could you possibly do anything so cruel, so wrong and wicked as to leave me?"

She knew that he was quoting her own words back at her. She wanted to stay with him because it had been an agony to have to run away.

Instinctively she put out her hands towards him and he took them in his.

"I am going to say now," he said very quietly, "something I swear to you I have never said to any other woman."

He looked at her for a long moment.

"I love you! *I love you*, Thea, as I never thought it would be possible for me to love any one."

Thea drew in her breath.

In a very small voice that he could hardly hear she whispered,

"I-I have – only just – realised that – what I am feeling for you – is *love*!"

CHAPTER FOUR

Thea was called in the morning by Valou's wife.

She was a large fat woman with what must once have been a very pretty face and an engaging smile.

She pulled back the curtains, put a cup of hot chocolate down beside the bed and said,

"It's a lovely mornin', *fraulein*, and it'll be hot later."

She brought in a can of hot water and put it on the wash-stand.

Later Thea went downstairs a little shyly. She had put on the skirt of her habit, but not the jacket.

As she expected, breakfast was laid on the balcony and Nikōs was already there waiting for her.

He looked, she thought, exceedingly handsome as he rose to his feet.

She then sat down beside him with a little murmur and Géza immediately brought her a steaming cup of coffee.

To her surprise there was also a dish of eggs, which was what her father always had at The Palace.

Nikōs must have known from her expression that it was not what she had expected for he said,

"I ordered something substantial to eat because we are going riding."

Thea's eyes lit up.

"That is what I would love to do."

"And so do I," he replied. "So hurry, because Mercury and Isten are waiting for us."

"Is that the name of your horse?" she asked.

"Yes, he is called after a very special God, who was worshipped by the Hungarians in the seventh century."

"I look forward to meeting him," Thea smiled.

"I am waiting to see how you ride," Nikōs replied with a broad smile.

She knew at once that he was teasing her, but at the same time she avoided meeting his eyes.

She thought that she had behaved last night in a very uncontrolled and foolish fashion. And she was sure that he was condemning her for not having more pride.

Then, as she finished her eggs, he said very quietly,

"I have not forgotten to tell you that you look very lovely this morning in the sunshine."

She looked away from him as he went on,

"You are very like the water lily buds we saw yesterday in the forest and I long, as I have never longed for anything, to see you in bloom!"

She thought that he meant when he would make love to her and she blushed.

Nikōs rose to his feet.

"Bring your jacket," he advised, "although I doubt if you will need it. The horses are waiting for us."

Thea ran upstairs, but, when she went to take down her jacket from the wardrobe where it was hanging, she had a better idea.

She thought that the jacket would get creased if it was attached to Mercury's saddle and it would be too constraining to wear if they were going to ride a long way.

Instead she opened a drawer to find the shawl that she had wrapped her clothes in when she had left The Palace. It was of a very fine wool and it had been beautifully knitted by one of the women in Gyula, who were noted for their considerable skill.

With a long fringe it was very graceful and, when she wore it, she felt that she was like the dancers who sometimes performed in the City.

She put the shawl over her arm and walked down the stairs.

Outside on the gravel drive at the back of the house the two horses were waiting for then somewhat impatiently

The moment Thea appeared Mercury gave a loud whinny of delight and nuzzled against her as he always did.

She patted him saying in a low and coaxing voice,

"How are you, my dearest? Are you rested? And did they give you plenty to eat?"

Valou laughed.

"He ate enough, Gracious Lady, enough for half-a-dozen horses."

"Thank you very much for taking such good care of him for me."

Then she looked at Nikōs's horse and gave a gasp of astonishment.

If Mercury was spectacular, so was Isten. He was a white stallion, over sixteen hands high and bigger than Mercury. There was no doubt that there was Arab blood in him and there was not a single patch of colour on the whole of his body.

Nikōs laughed at her surprise and he suggested,

"Let me introduce you to Isten, who is greatly enjoying your admiration."

"How can I find words to tell him how magnificent he is?" Thea commented.

"I am sure he can read your thoughts – as I do," Nikōs replied.

As he spoke, he lifted her gently into the saddle.

She felt a little thrill like sunshine running through her at the touch of his hands. And for a moment his face was very near to hers.

Having settled her in the saddle, he then arranged her skirt for her over the stirrup.

When it was completed to his satisfaction, he looked up at her.

Their eyes met and Thea was conscious of her love moving in her breast towards him.

Almost abruptly Nikōs turned away and swung himself onto Isten's back.

They moved off, riding away from the house and into the woods.

Because the path was a narrow one, Nikōs led the way and, after they had ridden for a little while between the trees, they began to descend.

It was down a twisting track into the valley.

He did not hurry and, when they reached the level ground below them, Thea could see that it was a perfect place for riding.

It was like the Steppes that she had galloped over yesterday and now she could ride side by side with Nikōs and, as she glanced at him, she realised that it was what he wanted too.

They urged their mounts forward and then they were galloping at an incredibly fast pace and speeding over the grassland.

Flights of butterflies rose in the air at their approach. And clouds of small birds flew out of their way.

The stallions, straining to keep up with each other, carried them faster and faster.

They galloped for nearly two miles before the stallions, as satisfied as they were, slowed down their pace.

Thea turned towards Nikōs.

Her cheeks were flushed and her eyes were shining as if the sun was captured in them.

"That was wonderful!" she cried. "Faster than I have ever ridden in my whole life."

"You ride exactly as I expected you would," Nikōs remarked.

"Like a Hungarian?" she laughed.

"Of course!" he agreed immediately. "I only hope that you will emulate some of their other characteristics!"

"Which one in particular?" Thea asked him lightly.

He did not reply, but, when she looked at him, she knew the answer.

How often, she wondered, had she heard people say,

"The Hungarians are the most passionate lovers in the world!"

She could not mistake the expression in Nikōs's eyes and quickly she looked away from him.

As they rode on, she was vividly conscious of how handsome he was and he sat on a horse better than any man she had ever seen.

She had always thought that Georgi was an exceptional rider, but Nikōs had an authority, at the same time an indefinable way of riding that seemed to make him become a part of his horse.

They rode on and Thea was utterly content to be riding with the man she loved as she had in her dreams.

There was no need to say even a single word.

She only knew that everything seemed more beautiful and more alive than it had ever been before.

The flowers seemed more colourful, the sky more blue, the haze on the horizon more magical and just because she was in love.

'How can I have been so foolish as to try to leave him?' she scolded herself.

As if she had spoken aloud, Nikōs said,

"It is something I will never allow you to do! I really cannot lose you, Thea."

There was a depth to his voice that made her quiver.

Because she was afraid of their becoming serious, she said laughingly,

"If you read my thoughts, there will be no reason for me to talk."

"Why should we," he asked, "when we can feel?"

She did not reply and he went on,

"I can feel you so vividly beside me that I know now what I have always missed in the past."

Thea drew in her breath.

"It was *you*!" he went on. "And now that we have found each other, you fill the whole of my world."

It was what she was thinking herself and she knew that love had suddenly changed the world as she knew it.

Now everything was dazzlingly irresistible and pulsating with life.

Equally it was so mysterious and magical that it was exactly what she expected from her Fairy stories.

They rode on and, as the sun rose higher in the sky and grew hotter, Thea began to feel thirsty.

"Where are — we going?" she asked him after a while.

She realised as she spoke that it was strange that she had not asked this question before, but it had not seemed to matter.

"I am taking you to enjoy a very different luncheon from the one you had yesterday," Nikōs replied.

She looked at him questioningly and he added,

"It is a surprise, but I think it is one you will really appreciate."

About half an hour later they turned into a thick wood.

Now there were no fir trees, but huge oaks, maples and ash and their branches were covered with spring leaves, a welcome protection from the rays of the sun.

The track between the trees was narrow and the low branches rubbed against them as they proceeded and once again Nikōs went ahead of Thea to lead the way.

There was no sound anywhere save for the song of the birds and the jingle of harnesses.

Thea thought that they must have reached the centre of the wood when they came to a clearing.

As she looked ahead, she gave a little exclamation of excitement.

In a circle under the protection of the trees there were a number of gypsy caravans.

Painted in brilliant colours, they looked almost like flowers and so did the women who ran eagerly to greet Nikōs. They spoke to him in Romany and he answered them in their own language.

Thea felt glad that she could understand what they were talking about.

"We privileged, honourable sir, very honoured you come to visit us again," they were saying, "but how you know we here?"

"A little bird told me," Nikōs replied and they laughed.

He then introduced Thea to them,

"This is a beautiful lady who is staying with me," he told them, "and she loves music!"

Thea felt her heart leap with anticipation.

She knew without being told that these were Hungarian gypsies. Although the gypsies came to visit Kostas, they more often came from the South where they would not be pure Hungarians.

Nikōs dismounted.

A gypsy boy took his stallion to where there was some lush grass for grazing and Nikōs lifted Thea from her saddle.

Once again she thrilled at his touch and she thought that he held her a little longer than was necessary before he set her on her feet on the ground.

She had already knotted the reins on Mercury's neck and without being led he followed Isten to where he could graze quietly.

"Now," Nikōs announced with a twinkle in his eyes, "we are hungry!"

As he spoke, he was looking at a pot that was suspended over a fire in the centre of the clearing.

Thea was already aware of a fragrant aroma coming from it and the gypsies brought out chairs for them.

One was the elaborate ceremonial chair where the Voivode Gypsy Chief would sit and the others were sometimes offered to an important guest.

The chairs were made mostly of stags' horns carved and decorated with pieces of gold and silver.

As she sat down, Thea thought that her chair was worthy of a Queen.

Then she thrust the thought from her mind. If she sat on a throne, it would be King Otho's.

She knew that, now she was in love, she would rather die than marry an old man.

If he tried to kiss her, as Nikōs had done, it would be an utter degradation that she could not contemplate.

Nikōs's hand was on hers.

"I will not let you look unhappy," he said in a low voice. "The gypsy music is full of love and that is exactly what I want you to feel."

She felt the sunshine invading her, because he was touching her hand and, when she looked into his eyes, she knew that he wanted to kiss her.

With an effort she forced herself to attend to the gypsy women.

They looked very attractive in their colourful gowns while coins that hung from the veils over their hair sparkled in the sunlight.

They brought Thea and Nikōs plates piled high with the stew that they had cooked over the fire.

As soon as Thea tasted it, she realised just how delicious it was.

She was certain that it was a mixture of roe deer, hare and partridge all in one stew and they had cooked it with herbs that grew naturally on the plain and in the woods.

While they were eating, the gypsies sat down on the ground at their feet.

They were then joined by the men who, with their high cheekbones, black eyes and jet-black hair, looked just as if they had come from the East.

That was true Thea remembered. The gypsies had originally come from India and had travelled West to Egypt and then on to Hungary and North to Russia.

When everyone had been served with the stew, the Voivode rose to his feet.

As he lifted his violin to his chin, there was silence.

At first he played alone and there was a passionate yet mystical note in his music.

Then gradually the other gypsies joined him.

A cymbal, a flageolet, bass, viola, cello and half-a-dozen violins blended harmoniously together.

To Thea it was sheer magic, as were the gypsies themselves. They had small, regular delicate features and sensitive mouths in their dark faces.

Their hands were long and slim and their limbs graceful, lithe and muscular.

The music changed from soft romantic tones to become the *Csdrdds*.

Thea had heard the music before, but never in such perfect surroundings or as well played as now.

It was a traditional Hungarian folklore dance and comprised all a gypsy's ambitions and fears and his passion for life that could become an intolerable sadness.

The bows of the gypsies were flashing over the strings of their violins and the music tumbled and fell before the pace accelerated again even stronger.

Thea felt as if she could not breathe and, as if Nikōs felt the same, he bent over to take her hand in his.

She knew then that the music was saying to her what was in his heart and it was telling her of his passion for her.

His love for her was wild, passionate and compelling and the sounds seemed to throb through her.

As the music rose up into the sky, she felt that it engulfed her and her feelings rose with it.

Her breath was now coming quickly from between her parted lips.

She felt her heart beating frantically in her breast and Nikōs's fingers tightened on hers.

He wanted to crush her against him and he wanted to kiss her so that she surrendered herself to him completely.

She knew by instinct that was what she wanted him to do.

The music came not only from the gypsies but from herself and it was linked with the music from Nikōs. It told her again and again that they were one indivisible person.

"*I love you*! You are mine!"

She did not know whether she heard Nikōs saying it in his deep voice or whether she listened to it with her heart.

She only knew her whole body as well as her mind was crying out to him.

"I – love you! *I love – you*!"

The music came to a sudden climax.

And then the wild movements slipped into a slow soft rhythm.

It gave Thea a chance to breathe again, but she knew that she had experienced something overwhelmingly emotional and passionate.

It was what Nikōs had wanted her to feel.

Then the gypsies were playing again and now several of the girls and young men began to dance.

It was very graceful and very beautiful dancing.

At the same time it was not the music of passion that had excited Thea in a way that she had never been excited before.

It made her shy to think of what she had felt.

She was now aware that Nikōs was watching her and she knew that he had brought her here because he had wanted her to feel as wild as the wind.

It was the sensation he had given her last night when he had kissed her neck and when he had held her completely captive with his lips.

She took her hand from his and clasped her fingers together.

She knew now that this was what she would feel if he made love to her as he had wanted to do last night.

'How – can I resist – him?' she asked herself.

Then she was ashamed of herself that she should think of anything so wrong and what her mother would say was a sin.

The gypsies' dance came to a sudden end and the dancers flung themselves down in an abandoned manner at Nikōs's feet.

"You are pleased, gracious sir?"

"Very pleased!" Nikōs replied with a wide smile on his face.

He brought his purse from his pocket and gave a coin to all those who had performed.

Thea thought that the coins were gold and she wondered if he was rich enough to afford it.

The gypsy girls kissed his hand, the men bowed and then thanked him.

"Now we must leave," Nikōs said firmly. "It is a long way home and the heat of the sun is over."

He looked up at the sky as he spoke and Thea realised that they had taken several hours eating, listening to the incredible music and watching the dancing.

It must now be getting on for four o'clock in the afternoon.

She called to Mercury and he came bounding up to her at once, while Isten was led by a gypsy boy to his Master.

Nikōs lifted Thea gently into the saddle.

She was still stirred by the music and she wanted to put her head on his shoulder and close her eyes.

She wished that he would take her back on the front of his saddle.

Instead she just said "thank you" in her soft voice. She felt that he would know that she was thanking him for everything that had happened today.

The gypsies started to cry out their farewells.

As they did so, the Voivode, who had played the violin first, picked it up again.

He started a gay romantic tune that seemed to have been composed especially to speed lovers on their journey.

Long after they were out of sight of the gypsy camp Thea could still hear the music in the distance.

She felt that it was carried to them by the movements of the leaves on the trees overhead.

Soon they were on flat ground and then they were galloping as they had on the way out, but not so wildly nor so swiftly.

Thea was sure that Nikōs was slowing his own pace so that she would not feel too tired.

They left the plain as they had before and rode up the twisting road that led them to the fir trees.

As they reached the top, Nikōs moved ahead of her.

Then Thea was suddenly aware of a number of men who came from behind the trees and encircled them.

Because her eyes were still dazzled by the light in the plain, she could hardly see them. They were little more than dark shadows.

Then she heard Nikōs speaking in a voice that she knew was one of hostility and with a stab of fear she realised that the men were bandits.

Everybody in Kostas knew of the dastardly gang of bandits that moved about the Balkan mountains. They were a serious menace to every country they visited.

They stole sheep and goats and horses were spirited away.

Often, it was whispered, young women vanished too and every Ruler, including her father, had tried to capture them.

But it always took time before the people in the City were aware of what they were doing to the farmers and stock breeders near the mountains.

By the time the soldiers came out to search for them, they had always vanished like the genie with the lamp.

Thea had heard so often what they looked like with their sheepskin capes, their strange hard faces and the threatening weapons that they carried in their waistbands.

She saw how their long, dark unruly hair was not covered with the exception of the man who, she thought, must be their leader.

He was speaking to Nikōs who was arguing with him and they were talking a different language to the one that Nikōs had used to Valou.

Thea did not at first understand them and then realised that the bandit spoke a mixture of Albanian, Greek and Turkish and she began to understand the sense of what was being said.

The Chief of the bandits was clearly demanding a ransom.

She knew then with a feeling of growing horror that they intended to take them prisoner.

She edged Mercury nearer to Nikōs. And as she did so she was aware of just how angry he was.

The bandit Chief then gave an order. Two men moved forward to hold onto the bridles of Isten and Mercury.

Immediately the horses reared.

"Don't touch our horses!" Nikōs called out sharply. "We will follow you, as we have no other choice."

"They not your horses for long!" the bandit Chief replied derisively. "They very good horses."

Nikōs did not reply, but Thea gave a cry of horror. How could she possibly let Mercury be taken from her by men like these?

She looked desperately at Nikōs and she could see how furious he was.

But he said to her quietly,

"We have to go with them, but it will be all right."

"How can it be?" Thea answered in terror.

Then she realised that he was speaking to her in English so that the bandits would not understand what was being said.

She had never imagined that he would be able to speak in English as she could.

She answered in a frightened little voice,

"What – can we do? How can – I lose – Mercury?"

"Trust me," Nikōs asserted firmly. "I should have anticipated that something like this might happen."

She knew that he felt helpless because he had no pistol with him.

She was aware, without his telling her so, that there was nothing he could do against a dozen bandits. And all the more so since she was with him.

If he had been alone, he might have somehow managed to gallop away from them and he could have taken the risk that they would not shoot at a horse as magnificent as Isten.

But it was a risk that he dare not take with Thea with him.

The bandit Chief was leading the way through the trees and with a sinking of her heart Thea recognised that it was in the opposite direction to Nikōs's house.

Now they were moving upwards into the mountains and they had to go slowly. It was a rocky surface and the horses might slip.

After what seemed a long time they came to a plateau of rock. The mountains towered above them, but there were caves on each side of the plateau and Thea realised that this was a perfect hiding place for the bandits.

As they appeared, other men, women and small children came running from the caves.

The men were all dressed in much the same way as the Chief with guns and daggers at their waists.

Some of the women wore bright vivid skirts like the peasants and they all wore brightly coloured headscarves and each woman was ornamented with a great deal of flashy jewellery.

Their huge earrings, bracelets and a variety of necklaces seemed strange against their dirty ragged garments.

They clustered around Thea, staring up at her on Mercury and she thought how different they were from the beauty and grace of the gypsies they had just left.

The bandit Chief said something to Nikōs and he dismounted slowly.

Then he lifted Thea down from the saddle and, as he did so, she clung to him whispering in English,

"Y-you will not – leave me?"

"Of course not."

She felt that, while he was reassuring her, he was at the same time becoming increasingly anxious.

The men would then have led Mercury away.

Nikōs stopped them sharply with a word of command and he took Thea's shawl from where it had been tied to the saddle and wrapped it round her shoulders.

She was glad of the warmth as they were now very high up in the mountains.

It was much cooler and she knew that it would be very cold later when darkness fell.

'How – can we – stay here? What – will they – do to us?' she asked herself frantically.

Because she was so afraid she slipped her hand into Nikōs's.

She felt his fingers, warm and strong, giving her a sense of protection.

Now they were standing in the centre of the plateau and the bandits were all clustered round them, staring at them as if they were wild animals rather than human beings.

Then the bandit Chief began to speak,

"You rich man," he said to Nikōs. "We want ten thousand ducats for you and five thousand ducats for your woman!"

He paused before he went on,

"You try escape or soldiers come, we kill. Each day we not receive money, we cut off one finger or one toe!"

Thea would have given a cry of horror, but the presence of Nikōs's fingers prevented her from doing so.

She knew again instinctively that he wanted her to be dignified and not let the bandits know that she was afraid.

She thought as well that it was how her father would expect her to appear in the face of adversity.

She could remember her mother saying to her,

"Royalty never show their emotions in public like ordinary people."

'I must – be Royal! I must be – *Royal*' she said to herself.

Yet she was trembling.

"What I will do," Nikōs was saying to the bandit Chief, "is to send a note to a friend who will give your messenger the money."

The bandit was listening.

"I will write the note in your language," Nikōs went on, "so that you can see that there are no tricks about it."

"If there tricks, you die!" the bandit Chief said fiercely.

Nikōs ignored him and searched in his pockets as if for something to write on.

The bandit Chief then gave an order and a man ran to bring him a piece of paper that was more like parchment that was none too clean and somewhat creased.

Thea suspected quietly that this was not the first time that the bandits had demanded a ransom.

When another man had provided an inkwell and a scruffy quill pen, she was absolutely sure of it.

There was a large rock at the side of the plateau and Nikōs stood at it to write. The ink was thin and the quill pen badly sharpened.

However he wrote slowly and distinctly.

Standing by him, Thea saw that he had put what was wanted into three lines.

Then he signed his name.

She thought as he wrote that at last she would learn his other name but he just signed the paper 'Nikōs'.

He waited for the ink to dry and he then turned the paper over on the other side and wrote the address that it was to be taken to.

Not knowing the country they were in, Thea had no idea whether it was far away or near.

She next thought with horror that they might be imprisoned for days or even weeks.

Then she remembered the threat that the bandit Chief had made and it made her want to cry out in sheer terror.

She managed, however, to stand stoically at Nikōs's side with her chin up.

Before he handed the bandit Chief the piece of paper, he read it aloud so that everybody could hear him.

He then read out the address and a young bandit came forward to take the paper from him.

"I hope you will hurry," Nikōs urged him.

"He hurry as I want money!" the bandit Chief interrupted before the messenger could reply.

"And now," Nikōs said, "as it will soon be getting cold, I would be grateful if we, as your prisoners, could be treated generously and be given a cave where we can be alone."

"You have cave," the bandit Chief replied. "Woman stay with us!"

Thea felt as if her heart had stopped beating.

While Nikōs was writing the note, she had been aware that some of the younger bandits had been pointing at her, laughing and whispering amongst themselves.

She thought they were just being rude or perhaps they were comparing her to their own women.

But now she was feeling afraid, desperately afraid!

Her hand went to Nikōs's and she knew as she touched him that he was as apprehensive as she was.

She was so panic-stricken that she contemplated running away and she would run into the wood, hoping that she would be able to hide in the undergrowth.

Then she knew that it was a hopeless idea and the bandits would be able to catch her easily and bring her back humiliated

They would be touching her and her whole body screamed out at the horror of it.

'Oh – God help – me!' she prayed.

Even as she did so, Nikōs had had an idea and perceptively she could see it come into his mind.

She was aware that he drew in his breath and was calling on some Power stronger than himself.

He seemed suddenly to grow in stature. He was taller, more authoritative and almost omnipotent.

She could not understand it.

Yet, because they were so closely attuned to each other, she knew that it had happened and Nikōs would save her.

He looked around at the bandits.

And then he said to their Chief,

"I have a story to tell you and I want you all to listen before it grows dark. Call all your people to come here and instruct them to sit down on the ground."

Thea thought that the bandit Chief was about to refuse him.

She could then feel Nikōs concentrating on him and he was willing him to be obedient to his will.

The two men gazed at each other, the bandit defiantly.

Without speaking but with a force that Thea could feel emanating out of him, Nikōs won the silent battle.

The bandit's eyes fell before his and he turned round and shouted at his followers.

They were gesticulating, pointing and talking amongst themselves, but obediently they came towards their leader and sat down as he commanded.

Nikōs did not move. He just stood with his arm round Thea's shoulders.

The men, women and children squatted until only their Chief was standing.

Thea was thinking that this could not truly be happening.

The rays of the dying sun were touching the peaks of the mountains and turning the snow to gold and even the rocks held a strange glow that was in itself very beautiful.

There was something unreal about the whole scene. The caves, the rocks, the frightening bandits and then themselves.

The situation was one of sheer terror.

Then Thea looked up at the sky and saw the first evening star. It was very faint, but it was there.

Thea knew, incredible though it might seem, that they were now protected.

It was by the power that Nikōs had just drawn into himself.

Nikōs was waiting.

As if he still had control over the Chief of the bandits, the man slowly and reluctantly sat down.

Then there was silence.

CHAPTER FIVE

Thea could feel the tension in the air.

The Chief of the bandits glared at Nikōs with what she thought was hatred and envy.

Certainly Nikōs looked very different from them and she was becoming increasingly aware that the younger bandits were watching her closely.

She found it difficult to force herself to ignore them, but she managed, however, to hold herself proudly.

Only Nikōs's arm around her gave a little comfort and she was praying fervently in her heart,

'Please – God – save me and Nikōs – please – *please*!'

She felt that her prayer was now winging its way up into Heaven.

Then Nikōs began to speak.

"I want to tell you a story," he started in his deep educated voice.

He was speaking the bandit's language, but Thea could quite easily understand all that he was saying.

"I married my wife, who is here with me, when she was fifteen. Because we were very much in love, we hoped that we would blessed with a child."

He glanced for a moment at the bandits' children. They might not be very prepossessing, but they were fat and well fed.

"Like all of you," Nikōs continued, "I wanted a son, but alas! We were not lucky."

He sighed and then went on,

"As the years passed, I began to be afraid that my name would die with me."

Thea now realised that the bandits were listening to him intently.

She felt that some of them looked rather more sympathetic than they had when Nikōs had started to speak.

"A few years ago in desperation," he was saying, "I prayed ardently to Héja, who, as you all know, lives on the highest mountain of this land and reigns over us all."

Thea had heard of Héja. He was the King of all the Gods in the mountains.

She realised by the expression on their faces that the bandits knew of him and doubtless worshipped him as well.

"I went to the Great Cascade," Nikōs went on, "which falls directly from Héja down into the plains to bring life and fertility to our crops."

One or two of the bandits murmured to themselves as if they were obviously familiar with the Cascade.

Thea thought vaguely that she had heard about it when she was a little girl.

She was, however, not at all certain which Kingdom it poured from the mountain tops into.

Nearly all of the Balkan countries boasted similar Cascades and she had the idea that the Cascade of Héja was thought more significant than the others.

"Then I had a dream," Nikōs carried on, "and I knew that Héja was speaking to me."

His voice rose,

"Héja told me that if, when the moon was full, my wife, Thea, bathed naked in the Cascade, she would conceive a child."

A sound of surprise came from the bandits and Thea herself was astonished.

"My wife is now with child," Nikōs declared dramatically "In five months I believe I shall have the son I require so urgently."

There was silence for a moment.

Then in a voice that sounded almost, Thea thought, like the roar of thunder he declaimed,

"It is Héja's child she carries! Héja, King of the Gods! If anyone should touch her, insult or defile her, they will be cursed for ever!"

There was a tense silence from the bandits and several of the women crossed themselves as if to protect themselves.

"You all know," Nikōs said, "the vengeance of the Gods, but you also know that they can bless and succour you."

His arm tightened round Thea as he added,

"You have been blessed because my beautiful wife, Thea, is here amongst you. Let her stay unmolested and in peace otherwise Héja will take a terrible revenge!"

Nikōs's voice rang out.

When he finally finished speaking, the sun had vanished below the horizon and the light faded rapidly from the snow on the mountain tops.

To Thea it seemed that they were now in almost total darkness.

Then, as if he must break the tension, the Chief bandit rose to his feet.

He gave an order and the bandits thrust thick tar-tipped sticks into the fire. And then there was light.

Nikōs and Thea did not move.

The bandit Chief addressed them in a surly tone,

"I show you cave where you wait till my messenger returns."

"Thank you," Nikōs said quietly.

He and Thea followed him across the plateau.

They had taken only a few steps when the women rushed forward carrying or dragging their small children with them.

They knelt down before Thea.

"Bless us," they begged, "give us the blessing of Héja."

For a moment Thea could only stare at them wide-eyed. Then Nikōs said quietly to her in English,

"Put your hand on their heads and say a prayer to each woman."

She was too frightened to do anything but obey him.

She touched the children's heads and as she did so, she said a simple prayer, which was one that her mother had always used when she prayed at her knee.

"May God and the angels bless you and watch over you now and for your whole life."

She soon had blessed all the children as there being not very many of them.

Then the women started beseeching her.

"I lost my last two babies," one cried. "Bless me that the next will be born strong."

Thea felt that what she was doing was almost sacrilegious.

She glanced at Nikōs.

"Pray that she will have a son. That is all she asks for," he suggested quietly.

Thea then put both her hands over the head of the woman.

"May God bless you and give you the son you long for, may he be strong, brave and at the same time kind and merciful."

The woman bent low and kissed Thea's feet.

Then Thea blessed the other women until Nikōs drew her away to where the Chief bandit was waiting for them.

She saw as they moved that the young men who had looked at her with lecherous eyes had now disappeared.

Nikōs had won.

The cave they were shown into was dark and rather intimidating.

One of the bandits' flares, however, was fixed outside, so that they could just about see.

There was a pile of dried leaves against one wall, the floor was sandy and Thea thought that there was a faint smell of chamois or perhaps it was a wolf.

But nothing mattered except that she would be with Nikōs and thanks to his presence of mind the bandits would not dare to touch her.

Then, as if they must show their gratitude, or perhaps their reverence, the bandit women came hurrying in.

They brought a woollen blanket to lay over the dried leaves.

It was none too clean, but at least, Thea thought, it would prevent their being pricked as she was certain that there would be brambles and thorns amongst the leaves.

There were two other blankets to cover themselves with. Also a rough pillow that looked more lumpy than soft.

The blankets were torn, but Thea was well aware that it was the best that they could do.

She thanked them a little hesitatingly in their own language and Nikōs thanked them too.

Then because it was now dark outside, the bandits withdrew and Thea knew that they were going to their caves to sleep.

The bandit Chief however said before he left,

"You try escape – we shoot you!"

It was as if he wanted to strongly assert himself, feeling that Nikōs's ascendancy over his followers had somehow humiliated him.

"We will be here when it is light," Nikōs replied.

With a sound that was like a grunt the bandit walked away.

It was then that Thea flung herself against Nikōs saying,

"You saved me – you were wonderful! How could – you be so – brave?"

He put his arms around her and replied quietly,

"We are safe for the moment, but I want you now to lie down and rest."

She looked at the bed and became aware as she did so that it was suddenly growing very cold outside.

Now that the sun had gone the temperature had dropped dramatically and she knew, because they were so high up, that deep snow was only just above them.

With what she thought was a note of amusement in his voice Nikōs said,

"I think, my darling, we would be very unwise if we did not rest close together."

"You – will not – leave me?" Thea stammered almost as if he had suggested it.

"That is something I shall not be allowed to do," Nikōs replied. "Instead, if I hold you in my arms, you will be warm and you will feel very much safer."

Because she knew that he was being sensible, Thea moved towards the bed.

It was more comfortable than she had expected.

As she lay against the side of the cave so that Nikōs would be on the outside, she found that she was actually quite warm.

The blankets were made of a thick wool from the mountain sheep.

She seemed to sink into the leaves beneath her and she was wearing her woollen shawl.

Only when Nikōs joined her did she remember for the first time that he was not wearing a coat.

He had expected to be back in the cosy warmth of his little house by this time and they would now be sitting in front of the log fire as they had done last night.

He lay down and put his arm around her and she said,

"I am afraid – you will be very – cold."

"I am relying on you to keep me warm," he replied.

He had spread the blankets over them up to their waists and now he pulled them even higher.

As he did so, Thea spread the end of her shawl across his chest, thinking even a little of its warmth was better than nothing.

Then Nikōs put his other arm around her and held her tight.

As she rested her head on his shoulder, she thought how she had wanted to be close to him like this.

It seemed extraordinary to her that it was the bandits who had made it possible.

"All that matters is that we are together," she surmised.

"Yes, we are together," Nikōs smiled as if he was reading her thoughts, "and you are not to be afraid, my darling one."

"I thought when you were speaking so cleverly that the bandits believed you," Thea said, "but if we had to die, at least I was with you."

"We are not going to die," he insisted in his deep voice. "We are both going to live, my precious, and we shall look back on this as an adventure that we will tell our children and our grandchildren."

Because she was shy, Thea gave a little murmur and turned her face against his chest.

She felt him kiss her hair and then he said very quietly,

"Will you marry me, my darling? I know now that I cannot live without you."

For a moment Thea was still.

That Nikōs should really want to marry her was the most incredible and yet the most marvellous thing that could ever happen to her.

She knew too that it was impossible and it was something that she would never be allowed to do.

Then she asked herself – why not?

If she was married to Nikōs, it would then be impossible for her to become King Otho's wife.

She was also aware that she could no longer be Royal and she knew how furious her father would be, but if she was legally married, there would be nothing in the whole world he could do about it.

She remembered what had happened to a distant cousin of hers.

She had been Royal, the youngest daughter of the King of Tek.

Her sisters, and there were three of them, were all married to reigning Monarchs, but she had fallen in love with one of her father's *aides-de-camp*.

They had run away together.

Her father, the King, had stripped her of her Royal rank and her name had been erased from the Royal Hierarchy.

Thea had been told that she was never spoken of again and she had often wondered if giving up everything as well as losing her Royal rank and status had been worth it.

Now she knew that if it was a choice between being a Princess and a Queen as the wife of King Otho or renouncing it all for Nikōs, there was no question as to what she would answer.

She loved Nikōs as he loved her.

They were closely attuned like the notes of two violins. They were incomplete without each other.

The thought flashed through her mind that if she was married to Nikōs, she need never go back to The Palace.

If the soldiers did not find her, then in time she would be presumed dead and then soon forgotten

If they did find her and she was married to Nikōs, there would be nothing that they could do about it anyway.

Except that she would no longer be *Princess* Sydel.

Nikōs was waiting for her to speak, but he did not move.

His lips did not touch hers, but she could hear his heart beating.

She raised her head to look up at him and she could see him in the light that came from the flare outside, which was now burning lower.

"I love – you!" she sighed.

"Then you will marry me?"

"I can – imagine nothing more – wonderful than to be – your wife!"

It was then she knew that he had been tense as he waited patiently for her answer.

Now their bodies seemed to melt into each other's and he held her so close that she could hardly breathe.

Then he said,

"That is what I wanted you to say and I swear to you, my lovely little Goddess, I will make you extremely happy."

"I love you!" Thea said again. "All I can think of is you – and your – love."

"That is all I would ever want you to think about and we will be married immediately we are free."

Thea gave a little shudder.

"You do – not think they will – hurt us?"

"Not if they receive the money they have asked for."

"There will be – no difficulty about – that?"

She was terribly afraid he might say that he had not have so much money, but he replied,

"Don't think about it, think only that in a very short while I shall be able to make love to you as I so want to do." ·

Thea thought of last night and blushed and she was glad that he could not see her face.

She wanted him to kiss her and she wanted him to give her the ecstasy and the rapture that she had felt before.

Foolishly, she mused, she had been frightened and had sent him away.

"When we are married," Nikōs now said, as if he was following his own train of thought, "I will teach you, my precious little Ice Maiden, all about love, but now you must be kind to me."

"Kind?" Thea asked.

"You know that I dare not kiss you."

"But – why not?"

She lifted her lips and knew that they were very close to his.

She wanted his kisses, she wanted them desperately and Nikōs's arms tightened.

"Last night," my darling one, "I frightened you and I knew afterwards that it was very stupid of me."

He drew in his breath before he added,

"You have no idea how beautiful you looked when I came to your bedroom with your amazing hair falling over your shoulders and your eyes green as emeralds in the light from the candles."

The way he spoke made Thea quiver.

As Nikōs was aware of it, he went on,

"Because we both have Hungarian blood in us, we come from the sun. We are easily aroused and our passions burn fiercely and demandingly like the heat of the sun itself!"

The way he was speaking was very exciting and Thea moved a little closer to him.

"I want you, my lovely one, I want you unbearably and uncontrollably. I want to kiss you from the top of your head to the toes of your tiny feet."

There was a note of wild passion in his voice.

It instantly reminded Thea of the music of the gypsies and she felt a flame awake within herself and move from her breast towards her lips.

"But because I will also revere and worship you as my wife," Nikōs continued, "I will not make you mine until we receive the Blessing of the Church and are joined by God in a bond that no man can sever."

The way he spoke was very powerful yet moving.

She felt her love seeping through her and her heart was beating frantically against his.

"Would it – matter very much if you just – kissed me?" she asked.

"You must not tempt me!"

"Tempt – you?"

"You don't understand," he said. "I adore your innocence and your ignorance about love, but I am also a man, Thea!"

'A magnificent and a heroic man,' she thought.

Who else would have shown such courage as he had shown when the bandits surrounded them?

Who else could have held them spellbound? Who else could have saved her from the degradation and horror of what they intended for her?

"You are – wonderful," she sighed. "So wonderful that I am afraid you will – find me dull as – your wife."

She thought then of the monotonous uneventful days and years that she had spent at The Palace.

The conversation of the Courtiers at Court was so dreary that she had ceased to listen to them.

With Nikōs everything had been a delight, exciting, stimulating and enthralling.

Now, closely held in his arms, even the bandits outside with their threats did not seem so intimidating.

Nikōs was holding her safe against him and in some strange way he seemed to have a dominance over them.

"What I want you to do," he was saying to her now and his voice was no longer vibrant with passion, "is to go to sleep. Tomorrow when the ransom has been paid, we will return home to our little house and arrange our marriage."

She knew that he was watching over her and because she loved him she must do as he asked.

"I will just say – my prayers," she whispered, "and – thank God that I am with – you."

She thought of how terrifying it would have been if she had been riding alone and then had encountered the bandits by herself.

They would certainly have taken her their prisoner if only because they wished to steal Mercury.

The younger bandits would have been waiting for her and, if Nikōs had not been there to save her, what might have happened?

She shivered.

"Forget it!" Nikōs urged her. "Forget everything except that the stars are watching over us."

"And Héja?" Thea enquired.

"He is the sublime King of all the Gods who dwell in the mountains," Nikōs replied, "and who knows that better than you, my perfect Goddess?"

He was teasing her and she gave a little laugh.

"After the way you spoke about him. I believe in him implicitly as the bandits do. How can they live up here and not be aware of the God above them?"

"They are in point of fact a very superstitious people," Nikōs explained.

"I know that – now and we – were very – lucky!"

"Very lucky indeed!" Nikōs said quietly. "And now, my darling, go to sleep."

"I am trying to do as you tell me, but it is incredibly exciting being so close to you."

"So how do you think I feel?" Nikōs enquired.

The passion was now back in his voice and, as if with a superhuman effort, he controlled himself and urged her,

"Go to sleep."

Thea said her prayers.

Then because she was very tired with all the emotions of last night and the happenings of the day, she gradually relaxed.

Nikōs could hear her breathing evenly.

The torch outside had finally burnt away and now there was only the light from the moon and the stars.

He looked through the opening in the cave at the rocks outside that the moon had turned to silver.

From the way he was lying he could just see some stars like diamonds shining in the sky.

He told himself that, whatever the difficulties ahead, he would protect and take care of Thea.

She was so beautiful.

And it was incredible that he had found the one woman in the whole world who was the completion of himself.

He was wise enough to know that it was almost an impossibility.

Yet he knew what Thea was thinking and she too seemed to know his thoughts.

There was an affinity between them that was nothing short of miraculous.

All through his life he had believed in a Power that had helped him when he needed it most.

He had called on it tonight when he had known better than Thea did what the bandits intended for her.

Women to them were of complete unimportance except for amusement and the breeding of sons.

Thea had heard of the bandits stealing away peasant girls from their homes and that was only part of the story.

Nikōs knew that many of the girls they carried away with them into the mountains were brutally ill-treated and they became half-mad with the dreadful terror of what they had been forced to endure.

Then they would either throw themselves down the mountainside or else were thrown into a chasm by the bandits themselves.

Only a few of their own women survived to cook for them and to tend them if they were wounded.

But they were of less importance than the mountain ponies that carried their ill-gotten gains.

That he had managed to save Thea was, he believed, a miracle.

It came from the God he believed in and who had never failed him.

What mattered in the future was that he had found Thea.

He loved her with an intensity that he had never thought possible and she had come into his life as swiftly as the starlight appeared in the sky at night.

He vowed silently that he would never lose her or let her leave him.

'She is mine!' he told himself over and over again.

He spoke fiercely as if he was fighting a battle for her.

*

Thea was asleep when she heard the sound of voices.

As she stirred and came back to consciousness, there was the sudden sound of gunfire.

She opened her eyes instantly and in horror.

As she did so, Nikōs took his arms from her and rose to his feet.

"What – is – happening?" Thea asked and she was now really afraid.

Nikōs straightened himself and the cave was just high enough for him to be able to stand upright.

The noise outside then increased.

Now through the opening of the cave Thea could see that dawn had broken and the sky was light.

Nikōs walked without hurrying to the entrance of the cave and looked out.

More shots were being fired and now the sound was almost deafening.

Thea sat up.

"I-I am afraid – oh, Nikōs – what is – happening outside?"

He turned back to her to say,

"Stay exactly where you are. Don't move whatever you do and don't look out, do you understand?"

It was an order that had to be obeyed.

Thea tried to collect her thoughts and to ask Nikōs again what was happening.

Then she saw him move forward and disappear.

She gave an involuntary cry of horror, but it was too late to stop him.

She was desperately afraid that, if the bandits were still shooting, they might shoot at him.

'Supposing,' she thought, 'if Nikōs is killed – and I am left here – alone?'

She wanted to run after him and to be sure that if, as she had thought before, he died, she would die too.

Now there were no more shots and without moving she thought that she could hear Nikōs's voice.

Then suddenly she could hear him clearly.

His voice was calm and authoritative and she knew that he was giving orders.

'What can be happening?' she asked herself again.

Because there was nothing else that she could do, she started to pray.

She prayed again desperately because she was so frightened.

'Please God – don't let them hurt him – please, God – keep him safe – I cannot lose him now – please, God – *please*!'

She closed her eyes and she was now afraid to listen.

At last, and it seemed to her a very long time, she heard somebody coming into the cave.

She opened her eyes and for a moment, because she was so frightened, it was impossible to see –

A man was blocking out the light.

Then she saw that it was Nikōs and she gave a cry of happiness and relief.

He bent down and lifted her off the bed where they had slept.

When he did so, he saw how pale she was and fear had made her eyes dark.

"It's all right, my darling," he said softly. "It's over and now we can go home."

"H-how – what – what has – happened?" Thea stuttered.

In answer to her question he drew her to the mouth of the cave. It was a few feet higher than the plateau.

She could see to her astonishment that there were soldiers everywhere, quite a large number of them. They looked very smart in their red coats in contrast to the scruffy bandits.

They now looked even more disreputable and unpleasant than they had the night before.

They were all being marched down the path that had brought Thea and Nikōs to the cave.

None of the bandits protested and Thea was sure that they had fired at the soldiers, who had fired back at them.

There were four bandits injured. They were lying or sitting on the plateau with blood on their legs, hands and arms.

Thea stood staring at what she could see.

Then with an inexpressible joy, she saw two soldiers leading Mercury and Isten.

"Mercury is – safe," she murmured.

"And so are you, my darling," Nikōs replied.

He helped her down from the cave and onto the plateau.

She went at once to Mercury and, as he nuzzled against her, she asked,

"You don't think they have hurt him?"

Nikōs asked the same question of the soldiers who shook their heads and replied,

"Only the saddles are damaged, *mein herr.*"

Thea looked at her saddle and she saw that the leather had been slashed. She supposed that the bandits had done so in order to look inside it.

"They were searching for money," Nikōs explained, "but I think it will carry you home."

He lifted her up as he spoke and placed her in the saddle.

Then he walked over the plateau and Thea could see there was an Officer superintending the removal of the bandits.

Nikōs talked to him for a long time and Thea could not hear what they were saying and she had no wish to.

She was patting Mercury and feeling incredibly happy that he was safe.

She knew just how agonising it would have been for her if he had been killed or hurt when the soldiers arrived.

She wondered how the soldiers could have learnt that this was where they were being held captive and she supposed that it must have been the ransom note that had told them.

At the same time she thought that the bandit who had carried it could not have gone very far.

She expected that Nikōs would explain everything to her later.

As she looked at him, thinking how handsome he was and how much she loved him, the sun rose.

The bandits had by now disappeared down the path she saw the Officer salute Nikōs and then hurry after his men and their prisoners.

Nikōs came back to her. He mounted Isten and thanked the soldier who had been holding him.

Then he smiled at Thea and suggested,

"Now we can ride home."

There was a note in his voice that told Thea how much it meant to him.

The little house on the side of a mountain would be their home, where she would live as his wife.

His eyes were on her lips and she felt as if he was kissing her.

Then with a feeling like the music of the birds in her breast she enthused,

"That is wonderful – absolutely – wonderful!"

CHAPTER SIX

They had ridden on a little way when Thea paused and looked back.

"There are — two soldiers behind us," she whispered nervously to Nikōs.

"I know," he answered. "The Officer insisted that we were seen home safely and I have also arranged for them to take our saddles to be repaired."

He spoke lightly, but Thea had the idea that he was glad to see that the soldiers were there and they would be in no further danger from bandits as they made their way to the little house.

She thought, although he did not say so, that Nikōs must be elated.

The bandits who had been such a menace for so long in the mountains had at last been captured.

She realised that the news would really delight her father and then she remembered that she would not be able to tell him about it.

In the fear and shock of hearing the fighting outside the cave, she had forgotten that last night she had promised to marry Nikōs.

Now it seeped through her like the sunshine streaming through the trees that she would be his wife.

Then once again she was recognising the penalties of making such a decision.

It made her shiver to think of how angry her father would be and he would undoubtedly find it extremely difficult to explain to King Otho exactly what had happened.

Yet she knew for certain in her heart that, whatever people might say about 'duty', love was stronger than anything else.

She loved Nikōs, she loved him with every breath she drew, and to leave him and to be without him would be a living Hell.

They rode on in silence until at last ahead of them she could see the little house.

Thea felt that the sunshine that had turned the windows to gold held a special message for her.

She knew instinctively that it was a welcome because she was coming back to the little house to stay.

They rode into the yard at the back of the house and, as Valou came running towards them, Nikōs said,

"Go into the house, my darling. I will just go and tell the soldiers what I want them to do about the saddles and then I will be joining you."

She had a strong feeling that he did not wish to have to explain to Valou that they had been captured by bandits.

She did as Nikōs told her and ran in through the front door and then up the stairs to her bedroom.

She thought, when she saw the beauty of it and the glowing colours on her bed, how different it was from where she had slept last night in that dark dank cave.

Yet all her life she would remember the joy and security of being close to Nikōs and the wonderful things he had said to her.

'I love him – *I love* – *him*!' she told herself over and over again.

She washed and changed her blouse for the other one that she had brought with her.

Then she hurried downstairs.

As she might have expected, breakfast was laid ready on the balcony table and Nikōs was waiting for her.

He rose as she walked towards him and she saw the love and happiness in his eyes.

Because she wanted to be sure that he was really there, she put out her hands towards him.

He raised them one after the other to his lips.

"We are safe – and we are – home," she murmured softly.

"We are home again, my precious," he replied, "and never again will I allow anything so horrible to happen to you."

His voice was caressing and she so wanted him to kiss her.

But at that moment Géza came out with a tray of their breakfast and a pot of hot coffee to go with it.

Thea sat down at the table and gazed in wonder at the exquisite view below them.

She thought at once that it was now even more beautiful and enchanting than it had been yesterday and the day before, but she knew that it was because her whole body was pulsating with happiness.

They ate at first in silence because they were both feeling hungry after their long ride.

Then Nikōs finally sat back in his chair and said,

"I have something to say to you."

Thea looked at him apprehensively.

He had spoken seriously and she was suddenly afraid that something was wrong.

"It is nothing frightening," he told her reassuringly, "in fact the very opposite."

Thea drew in her breath.

"I-I thought – perhaps you had – changed your mind," she said in a small voice.

"About marrying you?" Nikōs asked. "I swear to you that it will never happen, not until the stars fall from the sky and the seas run dry."

She gave a little laugh of sheer joy.

"What I want to say to you concerns our marriage," he went on.

Thea waited expectantly.

She thought now that perhaps she would have to confess to him who she really was.

But she was afraid that if she did so he might refuse to marry her.

He would know perhaps better than she did the penalties for renouncing her rank and for being an outcast among her own people.

Frantically she began to think of some name she could give him that was not her own.

She did realise that if she invented one it might render the marriage illegal.

Then she remembered that her father had a great number of titles and she thought that it was unlikely that Nikōs would have heard of them.

She felt sure that if she chose one that her father had never used, not even when he was travelling incognito, it should be safe.

As it was all passing through her mind, Nikōs said,

"I have been thinking, my darling, that, when we are married as I intend we shall be later this evening, it will be a very memorable day in both our lives."

"The most – wonderful day I could possibly imagine," Thea enthused at once.

"And for me it will be a glory out of this world."

He reached out as he spoke and took her hand in his.

"Because it means so much to both of us," he said, "I think it would perhaps spoil the wonder of it if we have to make tedious explanations to each other about our past."

Thea looked up at him with a puzzled expression on her face.

"The only thing that matters to us is the future," he went on, "when we will be together. I suggest therefore that from now on we think only of our love for each other and of nothing else."

Thea's fingers tightened on him as she replied,

"You mean – we don't need to explain exactly – who we are until later?"

"Much later," Nikōs responded, "when you are my wife and I have talked to you about something much more important, which is, my lovely one, *love*!"

The way he spoke made Thea feel again the ecstasy that she had felt yesterday when they had listened to the Voivode playing his violin.

"I think it is a – marvellous idea, but, if we are married simply as 'Nikōs' and 'Thea', will – it be valid – ?"

"I promise you," Nikōs answered that I intend to tie you to me with a legal bond as well as a spiritual one, which can never be broken!"

This was exactly what Thea wanted to hear.

At the same time it was an immeasurable relief not to have to explain who she was and why she had run away.

She thought that once again Nikōs was reading her thoughts and, without her telling him so, he knew that she was worried about her past.

They had this strange perception about each other and he was aware not only of what she felt but also of what was in her mind.

Nothing, she told herself, could be more perfect than that she should belong to him as his wife.

It would be foolish if their happiness, if not spoilt, could in any way be disturbed by the revelation that she was neglecting her duty in giving up her rank.

Her face was radiant as she enquired,

"When are we – going to be – married?"

"This afternoon when the sun will not be as hot as it will be earlier. And until then, my precious one, I want you to rest."

"I don't – want to – leave you."

"I have many arrangements to make," he said gently "and, as last night was also for me somewhat disturbed, I too intend to rest."

He gazed at her for a long moment before he added,

"I shall be thinking of you, loving you and counting the minutes until you are mine."

As he spoke, she saw the fire in his eyes and the colour rose in her cheeks.

Then she looked away from him and he said softly,

"I adore you when you blush and look shy. I don't believe any human being could be so attractive as well as so ethereal."

As Thea blushed again, he added,

"But you are not a human being and, for that matter, neither am I! We both belong to the Gods and to Héja, who saved us last night and will, I know, look after us tonight."

He raised her hand as he spoke and kissed it.

Then, because she knew that it was what he wanted after looking at him lovingly, she went indoors.

Only as she was taking off her very creased riding skirt did she remember that she had nothing to be married in.

She thought of all the beautiful gowns that filled her wardrobe at The Palace and she wished that Nikōs could see her in just one of them.

Then resolutely, because she wished to have no regrets, she told herself that it did not matter.

He would love her, whatever she wore, as she would love him.

She climbed into the comfortable bed.

As she did so, she thought that all the birds and the squirrels on the carved headboard welcomed her back.

She rested her head on the pillow and reckoned that she was very tired.

So much had happened and she felt too as if she had passed through every emotion that it was possible to feel.

She closed her eyes and tried to think only of the music of the gypsies and the note in Nikōs's voice when he had asked her to marry him.

'Tonight,' she whispered to herself, 'I shall – be his – wife!'

The sunshine was dancing dazzlingly in the room as she fell into a deep sleep.

*

Thea awoke suddenly and then realised after a moment that what had disturbed her was Valou's wife preparing her bath.

She could smell the fragrance of jasmine filling the air.

She sat up and asked her,

"What time is it?"

"Gettin' on for four o'clock, Gracious Lady," the woman answered, "and on the Master's orders, I bring you something to eat."

She brought in a tray and put it down beside the bed.

Thea saw that there was a bowl of cold soup, various fruits and a sponge cake as light as thistledown.

As she was eating, the woman came back into the room carrying something over her arm.

"What is that?" Thea asked her.

"Master tell me," the woman replied, "that you be married and we all very happy! Master often lonely here all by himself."

Thea thought that it was something he would never be again, but she was looking at what she now realised was a gown.

"Master say," Valou's wife carried on, "that you have nothin' to be married in. This, Gracious Lady, I make for my daughter. She marry next year."

Looking at what she held up Thea saw that it was a Wedding gown.

Girls in the Balkans started when very young to embroider their Wedding gowns, which were often masterpieces.

She could see that what Valou's wife was holding was as brilliant an example of local craftsmanship as the bed that she was lying in.

The gown was white. It was heavily embroidered round the hem of the full skirt with flowers of every colour.

The sleeves from the shoulder to the wrist and the low neck were a riot of wild flowers that bloomed in the grassland and in the woods.

It was beautiful and quite different from any gown that she had ever seen before.

"It is really lovely," she exclaimed. "But will your daughter mind if I wear it?"

"She very honoured, Gracious Lady."

Thea did not waste any more time.

She jumped from her bed and had her bath.

When she had dried herself, Valou's wife helped her into the Wedding gown.

It had been made for a girl who was not yet sixteen so it fitted her perfectly.

She knew as she looked at herself in the mirror that Nikōs would admire her.

It was like him, she thought, to remember that she would want to look beautiful on her Wedding Day.

When she had arranged her hair, Valou's wife brought her a wreath. It had a short tulle veil at the back and the flowers were freshly picked.

They looked very lovely against her red hair and she was sure that Nikōs had deliberately chosen them in white and blue.

When she was dressed and ready, she thanked Valou's wife and a little self-consciously walked down the stairs.

Nikōs was waiting for her in the sitting room and, when she entered it, she gave a little gasp of surprise.

He looked quite different and not at all what she thought of as himself.

He was dressed in conventional clothes that she had not seen him wear before.

The cravat at his neck was exquisitely tied and the only unconventional detail was the red sash he wore under his long-tailed coat.

It gave him a somewhat raffish appearance and Thea exclaimed,

"You look *very* – smart!"

"And you look exactly as I want you to," he said, "a Goddess from the mountains and the Queen of my heart!"

At the word 'Queen' Thea stiffened.

Then she told herself that it was the title that she really wanted and Nikōs was the King of her heart.

She moved towards him thinking that he would kiss her. Instead he put his hands on her shoulders and said in a serious voice,

"Are you quite certain, Heart of my Heart, that you will never regret marrying me?"

"How could I? It is what I want more than – anything else in the whole – world."

"I am giving you a last chance to escape," he said. "At the same time, if you try to do so, I am quite certain that I shall stop you. I could not let you go now!"

"All I – want is to stay – here with you for – ever," Thea sighed, "and to love you so that you will never become bored with me."

"That would be impossible," he answered. "Now we must go."

He took her to the door and she thought that there would be a carriage waiting outside for them.

To her surprise there was only Isten.

She saw that he had a new saddle and his harness had been decorated with flowers.

Valou was grinning when he saw them and Nikōs picked Thea up in his arms and sat her on the saddle. Then he mounted Isten behind her and, picking up the reins, rode into the wood.

Thea thought that this was the way that she had wanted to ride with Nikōs's arms around her, close to him and her lips very near to his.

She thought to herself that no man could look more handsome and at the same time so authoritative. It was the same way he had looked when he had forced the bandits to listen to him.

Because she was afraid that her feelings for him would overwhelm her, she managed to ask,

"Where – are we – going?"

"We are going to be married in a strange but delightful little Church," he told her, "which I hope you will come to love as much as I do."

"Is it in the wood?" Thea asked.

"It is in the wood," Nikōs affirmed, "and the Priest is a very old man whom I have known all my life."

He paused before he went on,

"He was offered a Bishopric, but because he loves the woods and the animals that live here amongst the trees, he came here to pray for them and for people who are too busy to pray for themselves."

As Nikōs spoke, they were moving slowly along a very narrow track and the sun shining through the fir trees threw shadows in odd patterns on the path.

As always when she was in a wood, Thea felt as if she was aware of the spirits that lived in it.

The goblins, burrowing under the ground and the Gods above them in the mountains.

As she had found Nikōs in the wood, she thought after centuries of searching for him, it was perfection that this was where she was to be married.

"That is what I think too," Nikōs said.

Thea gave a little laugh as once again they were knowing what each other was thinking.

Then ahead of her she saw the Church and knew that it was like no other Church that she had ever seen.

It was made of the trunks of trees and there were trees all around it, so that it seemed to be a part of them.

As they drew nearer, she could see that there was no glass in any of the windows.

Most of the Church was covered in creepers with small birds of every sort flying in and out of it.

There were also dozens of little red squirrels and running on the ground were rabbits and hares.

Nikōs brought Isten to a standstill and then a small boy came from the building to hold his bridle.

Nikōs dismounted and, lifting Thea down, said quietly,

"Now, my darling, our new life begins!"

He gave her his arm and they walked up the wooden steps into the Church.

It was empty save for a Priest standing in front of an exquisitely carved and coloured Altar.

As they moved up the aisle, Thea was aware of the soft movements of birds and animals and she felt because they were not frightened that they knew she loved them.

They were blessing her marriage in their own particular way.

As soon as they were in front of the Priest, he began the beautiful words of the Marriage Service.

When Nikōs made his vows in his deep serious voice, Thea knew how much it meant to him and she knew too how much he loved her.

As he placed a ring on her finger, she was saw at once that it was not the conventional Wedding ring. It was a superb signet ring that he must have been taken from his own hand.

She thought that later he would give her a traditional Wedding ring.

Yet she knew that the ring, which had been blessed by the Priest, would always be her most treasured possession.

As they knelt for the Blessing, Thea felt as if the whole Church was silent.

At the same time she and Nikōs were enveloped in a light that came not from the setting sun but from Heaven itself.

When the Service was over, Nikōs led her away and they left the old Priest kneeling in front of the Altar.

Thea felt sure that he was praying for their happiness and that they would never lose each other.

Isten was waiting for them outside and Nikōs gave the boy who held him a golden coin, which made him gasp with excitement.

As they rode away from the Church, he shouted out after them,

"Good luck! God bless you!"

And there was something very touching in his young vibrant voice.

It flashed through Thea's mind that perhaps one day it would be their son who called after them in similar words. And it made her blush to think of it.

As she turned her head so that she could rest it against his shoulder, Nikōs said,

"A strange Wedding, my darling one, but now you are mine for Eternity!"

Thea loved him so much that there were no words that she could think of to tell him so.

As if he understood her and was in a hurry to go back home, he urged Isten to move a little faster.

The sun was sinking low when they reached the little house and the sky was crimson and turning to gold.

The windows of the house reflected the sky and it seemed to Thea as if that too was part of the beauty of the whole world.

Valou took Isten from them and they walked into the house and went into the sitting room.

A log was burning in the fireplace and now there were great vases of flowers that had not been there before.

Nikōs closed the door behind them and then, before Thea was expecting it, his arms were around her.

"My wife!" he murmured quietly.

Then his lips were on hers.

As he kissed her the rapture that she had felt before seemed to seep through her and the intensity of it made her feel as if he carried her into the heart of the sun.

She realised that his kiss was passionate and demanding but equally there was something very spiritual about it.

She sensed that the beauty of the Service in the little Church in the woods still lingered in his heart and mind.

He kissed her as if he owned her and at the same time there was a reverence about his love and it was what she too felt for him.

She not only loved him as a man who had so completely captured her heart, she also admired him because he was so fine and noble and she knew too that he was good.

She thought perhaps that 'good' was an odd word to apply to him.

Yet there was no other word that could express what she felt and was in some way linked with everything that she believed in.

Nikōs kissed her until they were both breathless.

Then, as the sun that had been coming through the windows died away and it was dusk, he said,

"Come and have something to eat, my beloved. It is waiting for us next door."

They went into the dining room and she was not surprised to see that it too was decorated with cascades of flowers that were all white.

The table was beautifully arranged, but there was nobody to wait on them.

As Thea looked at the sideboard, she realised that Valou's wife must have been cooking for them all day.

"How can we eat so much?" she laughed.

"Valou and his wife will be very disappointed if we do not," Nikōs answered.

He kissed her lightly as he spoke.

Then he chose without her telling him what she would eat and put the plate down on the table.

"I am too excited to be hungry," Thea announced.

"So am I," he answered, "but they have gone to so much trouble."

She realised that he was only making it an excuse to make her eat.

She did try, but afterwards she could not remember what she had eaten.

She was only acutely aware of Nikōs looking so handsome and so different from the way he had looked before with his artist's bow tie and his velvet jacket.

There was champagne for them to drink, but she felt that it would be impossible to feel more elated than she did at the moment.

Nikōs raised his glass to her.

"To the most beautiful woman I have ever seen in this world!" he toasted. "Someone so perfect in every way that I find it hard to believe that at last she belongs to me."

"You sound as if you have been waiting for me for a long time," Thea teased, "and I know that people would be shocked if they knew the truth."

"The truth is quite simple," Nikōs answered. "I have been searching for you in this life and, I think, in a million other lives before I found you and now I will never let you go."

"Do you think I would want to?" Thea asked him.

"I have fought more than a thousand battles for you, I have sailed across a hundred seas and climbed the highest mountains in the world to find you."

"I know – now that I have been – looking for you too," Thea answered. "You were in my dreams – but when I awoke you were gone."

"Now I will always be there and I think we both realised in the Church in the wood that love is found in unusual places and not always in those that are conventional."

Thea thought of her father's plans for her and knew at once that Nikōs was right.

The love they had found had nothing to do with this mundane world. It was spiritual and belonged to the trees, the birds, the flowers, the sun and the stars.

They finished their meal and Thea had managed to eat more of the delicious food than she had expected to at first.

Then when Thea thought that they would return to the sitting room to sit in front of the fire, Nikōs drew her tenderly up the stairs.

As he did so, she felt her heart begin to beat excitedly and she could feel his need of her vibrating from him.

They reached the top of the staircase.

He turned to the room on the other side of the corridor to hers, which she had not seen before.

He opened the door and for a moment she felt that she must be dreaming.

It was so different, so entirely different from anything that she had expected from any bedroom that she had ever seen.

As she looked round, she realised that the walls were all hung with material.

On it Nikōs had painted the colourful flowers that meant so much to them both and the birds that they had just left behind in the wood.

It made the room look as if they had stepped onto the flower-filled grass where they galloped their horses.

There were flowers of every colour flaming round them.

It was so beautiful that Thea could only stare at it in bewilderment.

"I think, my precious," Nikōs pointed out, "that, when I painted this, I was thinking of you."

"It is *so* beautiful!"

"And that is why you need the right background for me to tell you how much I love you."

Now Thea could see the bed, which was very low on the floor and it was carved in the same way as her own.

The difference was that the headboard was decorated entirely with butterflies. Large ones and small ones, they flew open-winged to blend with the flowers on the walls.

"How can you have thought of anything so – wonderful?" she gasped.

"I told you – I was thinking of you."

Nikōs put his arms around her.

She realised that, while she had been looking at the room, he had pulled off his coat and his cravat.

Now in his thin white shirt and the red sash above his trousers he looked, she thought, even more exciting than he had before.

Because she felt shy she said a little incoherently,

"I-I have not yet – thanked you for – thinking of my – Wedding gown."

"You look adorable in it," Nikōs replied. "But now I want you closer to me and I want to see your glorious hair over your perfect white shoulders."

He took off her wreath as he spoke.

Then he pulled her close into his arms and kissed her.

She was trembling with the excitement that was flickering through her like little flames.

He lifted her arms and her Wedding gown slipped onto the floor and he carried her naked to the bed.

He put her down and, as she looked up at the ceiling, she saw that it depicted the sky.

One half of it was blue and brilliant with sunshine and the other half was filled with stars.

She knew, now that the sun had set, the real stars would be shining above them in the sky.

And yet here in this bedroom, Nikōs had somehow captured the world that mattered to them.

A world of beauty, music and birds.

Even as she thought of it, she heard the soft sound of the Voivode's violin.

For a moment she thought again that she must be dreaming.

Then she realised that Nikōs was playing the same ecstatic music that had moved her so emotionally the day before.

As the melody throbbed with a passion that aroused her Hungarian blood, Nikōs joined her.

He blew out the candles that had illuminated the room before he did so.

To her astonishment there was a faint light behind the silken walls and in the ceiling overhead.

She did not ask him how it was done, she only knew that it was very lovely, unusual, original and so thrilling that it completed the wonder of the world that contained just them alone.

No one could encroach on them at this moment in time and space and no one could hurt them.

She knew that what Nikōs had said was true – they were protected by the Gods.

Then he was kissing her eyes, her nose, her lips and the softness of her neck.

It made her tremble.

And then she could feel a wild passion that was irresistibly demanding seep through her.

It was the ecstasy of Nikōs's kisses.

His hands moving over the softness of her skin.

His heart beating against hers.

The music swirled and rose as if the notes themselves flew up to the stars and touched the moon.

Thea knew that her heart and soul went with the music.

"I worship you," Nikōs murmured.

His voice was part of the music, which was becoming more and more intense.

Now there was a wildness and an irresistible desire.

Thea felt a longing within herself that she could not control.

She loved Nikōs absolutely and completely. She wanted to be even closer to him than she was at this very moment.

She did not understand and yet she wanted to give him herself.

She wanted to be his and no longer have any identity of her own.

"I love you – oh, Nikōs – I love you!"

She was not certain whether she said the word aloud, they came from the rapture that he was giving her.

"You are mine!" he asserted. "*Mine*, Thea, as you were meant to be since the beginning of time!"

"I am – yours! I – want to be yours – and oh – Nikōs – *I love you!*"

The music rose higher and higher and was carrying them together towards the stars.

She could feel the fire on Nikōs's lips and the fire within her breast.

The world was left behind.

There was nothing except their love and they were one person.

*

It was a long time later when the Voivode was no longer playing and the light behind the curtains was a soft glow that Thea whispered to Nikōs,

"I-I did not know that – love was like this."

"Like what?" Nikōs asked.

He drew her a little closer to him and his lips were on her hair.

"It – it belongs to – God," Thea murmured, "and it is also – everything that I believe in and sensed was there – if only I could find it."

She was thinking as she spoke of the woods and of her dreams.

She was seeing, as if she was now sitting beside it, the lake where she had found Nikōs on that very first day.

"We have been very privileged," he said quietly. "The Gods have blessed us and we must never cease to thank them for their generous bounty."

"How could I do anything else – now that I am your wife?" Thea asked.

She gave a deep sigh.

"I never dreamt I should find anyone so – marvellous, but – somehow – I knew you were there waiting for me."

"And I feel the same," Nikōs smiled, "but I was desperately afraid that my dreams would never come true."

"And now that they – have?" Thea asked.

"I have to make sure that I am not dreaming!"

Because he was touching her, she gave a little murmur.

"How is it possible," he asked, "that you can be so lovely, so beautiful and so perfect in every way?"

"That is what I – want you to think – but I am a little afraid you may be – disillusioned."

"That is something I will never be. I know that only you, my darling wonderful little wife, could have married me as you have without explanations and without having anyone you belong to at the Wedding Service."

"I-I don't want to – think about it," Thea said. "Tonight there is – nobody in the whole – world but you!"

"For me," Nikōs replied, "you fill the sky. I know that, if anybody is missing you, it is the Gods in the mountains above us."

"When you – loved me," Thea said in a low voice, "I felt as if we were – one with the Gods – and no longer human."

"I thought the same," Nikōs answered. "And now that my Ice Maiden has melted, I am no longer afraid that she will go back to the snow!"

Thea gave a little choked laugh and hid her face against his neck.

"Are you – shocked that I was – so excited by you?" she asked.

"How could I be shocked by my own Hungarian blood?" Nikōs replied. "And I still have a great deal to teach you about love, my precious wife."

"That – is what I – want and only you could have thought of the music which makes me feel very – Hungarian!"

"I am only afraid that I might have disappointed you."

She knew that he was teasing her and she said passionately,

"You are – everything they have ever – said about Hungarians and now I know what the word 'lover' really means."

Then Nikōs was kissing her again.

Once more her whole body seemed to be filled with fire as she responded to him.

She was not sure whether the Voivode's music was still playing outside or whether she heard it in her heart.

But there was music rising to a thrilling crescendo.

As Nikōs made her his, they were once again touching the stars.

CHAPTER SEVEN

Nikōs climbed out of bed and pulled back the painted curtains so that the sunshine could stream into the room.

There were two windows when the curtains were drawn back with one looking over the woods and one over the valley.

Thea saw him silhouetted against the morning sky and she thought that no one could be more attractive and no man more masculine.

"Do you realise, darling," she asked in a soft voice, "that we have now been married for four days?"

"I am not certain," Nikōs replied, "whether it feels like four centuries or four hours!"

He was teasing her and she laughed.

Then he came back to look at her with her red hair falling in cascades over her shoulders and the painted butterflies behind her seemed part of her green eyes.

"I wonder if you realise how lovely you are?" he asked now in his deep voice.

"Tell me," she urged him.

She put out her hands to him and he said,

"You are tempting me, but while I want to get back into bed and hold you tight, I have to get up."

There was something in the way he spoke that made Thea look at him apprehensively.

"Why?" she asked after a moment.

She thought that he was feeling for words before he responded,

"Ever since we have been married, my precious, everything we have done together has been so rapturous and so unbelievably marvellous that all I really want to do is to stay here for ever, telling you how perfect you are!"

"That is – what I want too," Thea sighed.

Then because her instinct told her that there was something else in his mind, she asked nervously,

"What has – happened? What is – wrong?"

"There is nothing wrong," Nikōs said. "But I knew, my darling, that we would have to face the world one day and unfortunately it is *today*."

"Today?" Thea asked. What do – you – mean?"

He climbed into bed, put his arms around her and pulled her close to him.

"I don't want you to be frightened," he said. "At the same time I want you to do what I ask of you."

He felt a little tremor run through Thea's body before she replied,

"You know because I love you so much that I will do – anything you ask, but now – I am frightened."

"It may seem frightening," Nikōs said, "but I want you to trust me."

She remembered that he had said the same when they were being taken prisoner by the bandits.

"You know I trust you," she asserted passionately, "and I love and adore you. No man could be more utterly and completely wonderful."

Nikōs's arms tightened and then, as if he forced himself to speak, he said,

"I have received a message that makes it imperative for me to see my family as soon as it possible for me to do so."

Thea drew in her breath and stifled a cry of horror.

"I think therefore," Nikōs went on, "while I tell my family about you, you must tell yours about me."

"T-tell my — family?" Thea faltered.

Nikōs smiled.

"I suppose sooner or later we have to be frank with each other. It seems just incredible that I have no idea what your name was before you became my wife!"

"Does it — matter?" Thea asked.

"It is something we both have to do sooner or later," Nikōs replied to her quietly.

There was a long silence and Thea knew that he was willing her to do what he wished.

Because she could not bear to disappoint him, she said after a moment in a very small voice,

"What — am I to do?"

"I want you to tell them," Nikōs replied, "and I think, my darling, that you came here from Gyula."

He saw Thea start and he went on,

"Tomorrow, after I have arranged everything and done what I have to do, I will come to Gyula and meet your father and mother."

Now Thea did give a little cry of protest and Nikōs urged her,

"Don't be afraid. If they are angry, I will placate them. Don't tell them tonight that we are married, but leave me to bear the brunt of their anger."

"They will be – *furious*!" Thea muttered.

"Just make your apologies for having been away for so long," Nikōs answered, "and trust me to do what is right when I arrive."

"How – how will you know where to – find me?" Thea asked.

As she spoke, she knew that she was shrinking from telling him who she was.

If he was going away from her, perhaps when he had time to think it over, and she was not there, he would be sorry that they were married.

"Leave everything until tomorrow," Nikōs stressed as if he read her thoughts.

He thought for a moment and then he said,

"Meet me outside the town on the main road and then we will go together to confess what has happened and hope that your family will forgive us."

He smiled as he spoke, but Thea wanted to say that it was no laughing matter for her.

She could imagine the contempt that her father would treat any commoner with when she had married.

She had a vision of them both being thrown out of The Palace and humiliated in front of the Courtiers and the servants.

Then, as if everything was decided, Nikōs turned her face up to his and kissed her.

For a moment, because she was perturbed, she did not respond until inevitably she felt her heart throbbing with excitement.

The flames of sunshine ignited within her and became fire.

Then, as the sun came flooding in to turn Thea's hair to a shining glory, everything else was forgotten.

Nikōs was kissing her and touching her and just how was it possible for her to think of anything else?

Her whole body responded to his and they were suddenly in a dream world.

There were only themselves and the beauty of the Gods.

*

Thea rode over the grassland.

She knew that within a few minutes she would have her first sight of the City and The Palace white and majestic standing above it.

She had the terrifying feeling that she was leaving all her happiness behind her.

Nikōs, before he saw her off, had held her close in his arms.

"You are not to be frightened," he ordered, "you are to concentrate on our love and know that, because you are my wife, no one can ever take you from me."

"Y-you are – sure of that?"

"Absolutely certain," he affirmed. "Once again, my perfect little wife, I ask you to trust me."

He kissed her until she knew that she would have gone down into Hell itself if he had asked her to do so.

When she had ridden away, she did not look back, because it might be unlucky.

She was aware that Isten was waiting for Nikōs and also he was dressed in conventional riding clothes. Again his artist's bow had been discarded and his white stock was neatly tied around his neck.

His polished riding boots shone like mirrors.

She clung to him, terrified that once they were parted she would never see him again.

"You – will be – safe?" she asked in a trembling little voice.

"I promise you there will be no dragons, no bandits and nothing to harm me until I come to you tomorrow."

"At what time?"

He thought for a moment and then he answered,

"At about four o'clock. Where will you meet me?"

"In the meadowland that is just before you reach the bridge that leads into the City," she replied.

"You promise me you will be there?"

"That is the question – I was going to ask you," she countered.

He kissed her again and lifted her up onto Mercury's back and she rode away.

'I love him! *I love him*!' she said over and over again to herself.

She was still saying it three hours later as she crossed the bridge where she would meet him tomorrow.

She rode back to The Palace and, when she entered through the main gate, the sentries came to attention.

She was sure that they were looking at her with curiosity and she felt certain that by this time everybody in The Palace would be aware that she had disappeared.

Because she was so nervous, she did not go up to the front door but rode round to the stables.

The Head Groom came hurrying out of his workshop as soon as he saw her.

"Your Royal Highness!" he exclaimed. "You're back! Everyone's been ever so worried about you in case you'd had an accident."

He looked at Mercury with admiration and Thea said,

"No, we are both quite safe."

She dismounted and walked into The Palace by a side door.

She went upstairs to her bedroom and rang for her maid.

"Your Royal Highness!" Martha cried. "Just how can you have given us such a fright? Where have you been?"

While she was changing her clothes, Martha was reprimanding her as she had when she was a little girl and it was all so familiar.

She still had to face her father, however, and she was well aware that it was going to be a difficult confrontation.

At this time of the day he would be in one of the State rooms dealing with the affairs of the nation and surrounded by his Statesmen and *aides-de-camp*.

But she went first to see her mother.

The Queen, who was never in very good health, was resting in one of the window seats of the drawing room.

She gave an exclamation of surprise when she saw Thea and then asked her,

"Dearest, where have you been? We have been so worried and your father is very angry. I became dreadfully apprehensive when we would never find you."

"I am sorry, Mama, if I have upset you, but I think you can guess why I ran away."

The Queen sighed.

"I knew only too well that you had no wish to marry King Otho and, when I saw him, I could understand exactly what you were feeling."

Her mother was so kind that Thea felt the tears come into her eyes.

"I am sorry, Mama, but I could not marry an old man like him."

"I know, dearest, but your father thought that it would be for the good of our country."

"Is he still very angry?"

"He was at first," the Queen replied, "then he thought that you must have had a nasty accident. Yesterday he sent out some more Officers we can trust to look for you, but they came back in the evening to say that, although they had ridden for a long way, they could not find you."

The Queen smiled.

"I thought you would be with one of your old Governesses, but Papa did not think of that, so I did not suggest that was where they might look."

Thea laughed.

"Oh, Mama, you are so kind and you *do* understand what I was feeling."

The Queen sighed again.

"It is the penalty for being Royal."

"Does Papa still expect me to marry King Otho?"

The Queen looked at the door as if she did not wish to be overheard and then she said,

"He has not told me so, but I have the idea that he has by now realised the impossibility of such a marriage. Try not to upset him now that you are back."

Thea kissed her mother again and then went to find her father.

Because it was nearly luncheontime, she thought that he would have gone into his study in their part of The Palace.

She was right and, when she slowly opened the door of the study, he was standing at the window gazing out onto the flower garden.

"Good morning, Papa."

He turned sharply when she spoke and she saw an expression not of anger but of relief on his face.

"Thea, you are back!"

She ran towards him, put her arms around his neck and kissed his cheek.

"I am sorry, Papa, if I have upset you."

"Where have you been, you naughty girl? I thought you might have had an accident or been in danger of some sort."

Thea knew that this was true, but she had already decided that she would not tell him about the bandits.

"I am back now," she stated, "and I am very sorry if I worried you so much, Papa."

"I am really very angry," the King insisted.

But there was a note in his voice that was more like relief than anger.

In fact they were all so relieved that she was home that, rather surprisingly, they did not question her as to where she had been.

They had all accepted her mother's supposition that she had been with one of her old Governesses.

Only after dinner, when they talked about everything that was happening in Kostas and read Georgi's letters did Thea finally relax.

It had all passed off so much better than she had dared to hope.

Yet she wondered what they would feel tomorrow when she confessed that she had been married to a commoner without their permission.

'Perhaps they will forgive me,' she thought hopefully.

Then she knew, as far as her father was concerned, that was most unlikely.

Because her mother always went to bed early, Thea retired to her bedroom soon after dinner was finished.

"Goodnight, Mama," Thea said, kissing her affectionately.

"Goodnight, my dearest, I am so happy to have you home again."

Her father said much the same and this made Thea feel even guiltier.

"I shall have a great deal more to say to you tomorrow," the King added, "and no more naughtiness, do you understand?"

"Yes, Papa."

"That is a good girl. The Palace seems very empty when you are not here."

Thea drew in her breath and as she went up to her bedroom, she wondered how she could bear to hurt them.

Then she knew that nothing mattered except for Nikōs.

She belonged to him and she was part of him.

Perhaps one day they would forgive her, especially if she had a baby who would be their grandchild.

It was a long time before she went to sleep and she kept thinking that even her mother would find it hard to sympathise with her when she learned of the way that she had behaved.

'Help me, *help me*,' Thea found herself praying to God, who had blessed their marriage.

She also prayed to Héja even though he was not worshipped by the people of Kostas.

But he was a God of the country that Nikōs belonged to and she knew that in the future he would play a very special part in her life.

Finally she drifted off to asleep, wanting the night to pass quickly so that she could be with Nikōs again.

She had told her maid, Martha, not to call her very early as she had known that the long ride home and her anxiety as to how her father would react to her return had made her feel exhausted.

She wanted, above all else, to look beautiful for Nikos when he arrived at The Palace.

She planned which of her prettiest riding habits she would wear.

She knew as she did so that she was really afraid that when he came home that there was someone beautiful whom he had known before to greet him.

Or perhaps there was somebody whom his family wanted him to marry rather than an unknown young woman he had met in the woods.

She was still asleep and dreaming of Nikōs when she was awakened by Martha coming into the room.

She thought it was annoying that she had come so early in the morning and turned over hoping that she would then go away.

But, having drawn back the curtains, Martha came to the side of her bed to say,

"You must wake up, Your Royal Highness."

For a moment Thea pretended not to hear her and then Martha repeated,

"His Majesty says it's real important you're downstairs in half an hour."

Thea sighed and opened her eyes.

"But why? What is the time?" she enquired.

"It's nearly twelve noon, Your Royal Highness and His Majesty says he has a special guest comin' to luncheon whom you are to meet."

Thea sat up and wondered why her father had not told her about this special guest last night.

She just hoped that it would not entail one of the long-drawn-out State luncheons, which would make her late for Nikōs.

She climbed out of bed and quickly had her bath.

She had planned to put on her riding habit so that she could leave without having to change again.

But, as there was a special guest, she allowed Martha to dress her in one of her prettiest gowns.

It was of a very pale green that made her think of the woods where she had met Nikōs.

It was made in the latest style, swept to the back with a large bustle and it made her skin look dazzlingly white and her hair even more fiery than it was usually.

She wore a small necklace of emeralds that matched her gown and there was a bracelet to go with it.

She did not take long in dressing and she told Martha to put her riding habit ready so that she could change swiftly after luncheon was over.

She had chosen one of a very pale blue, which was the colour of the flowers that she had worn in her wreath when she was married.

She decided that this afternoon she would wear a riding hat as Nikōs had never seen her in a hat.

Then because time was getting on and Martha was fussing over her, she hurried from her bedroom.

She ran along the corridors to the main part of The Palace.

There seemed to be more footmen about than usual in the hall and also a number of the more elderly Courtiers.

She was now wondering who the special guest could be.

She found her father, as she had expected, in the salon, which was next door to the main dining room.

It was where he and her mother always received their more important guests.

It was an impressive room with a great deal of gold decoration. Fortunately the walls were white and the carpet was blue, so that the Royal crimson did not clash with Thea's hair.

As she kissed her father and mother, she saw that they were specially dressed for the occasion.

"Who is this important guest, Papa?" she asked.

"It is King Árpád of Levád," her mother said before the King could speak, "and he proposed the visit himself."

"Of Levád?" Thea repeated and wrinkled her forehead.

"He has never been on a visit to Kostas before," the King explained, "and naturally we are delighted to welcome him."

There was something in the way her father spoke and the way he looked at her that made Thea feel as if a cold hand clutched at her heart.

She remembered that King Árpád with the exception of the old King Otho was the only unmarried King in the Balkans.

She knew now exactly what her father was planning and wanted to tell him immediately that such an idea was out of the question.

Then she remembered what Georgi had told her, that King Árpád was a misogynist and disliked women.

Perhaps he had changed his mind, but whether he had or not, it was too late.

She had, however, no wish to be alone without Nikōs beside her when she said so.

"I must say that I have never met the man," her father was saying, "although, of course, I knew his father. Levád is a large and important country. One of its boundaries marches with ours."

"Georgi told – me," Thea began in a small voice, "that King Á – "

Before she could finish the sentence there was the sound of voices and the double doors at the end of the salon were flung open.

The Courtiers who had been waiting in the hall now advanced towards them.

Her father and mother then moved away from her and Thea was left alone in the middle of the room.

She knew that she ought to follow them, but for a moment she contemplated leaving the salon by another door and running away into the garden.

Then she told herself firmly that there was no need to be afraid.

She was married to Nikōs, she was his wife and, whatever schemes her father might be hatching for her to marry King Árpád, they would come to nothing.

She closed her eyes for a moment and thought that she could hear Nikōs saying in his deep voice,

"*Trust me.*"

'He will make everything all right,' she told herself.

She was sure that nothing and nobody could undo the sacredness of the vows that they had made to each other in the little Church in the wood.

Her father and mother had greeted the King and were talking with him by the door of the salon.

It was then, slowly and reluctantly, knowing that it was her duty Thea moved towards them.

As she did so, she was saying in her heart,

"Oh, Nikōs, I love you! *I love you!*"

She was sending her thoughts rapidly towards him so that he would come and rescue her.

"And now, Your Majesty," she heard her father say, "I would like to present to you my daughter, Sydel."

"I should be delighted," a deep voice replied.

Thea had already sunk down in a deep curtsey.

Then, as the King took her hand in his, she felt a strange tingling sensation.

It was so vivid that involuntarily she looked up at him.

Suddenly she was stunned into immobility.

It was *Nikōs* who stood there!

Nikōs wearing a smart uniform covered with decorations.

Nikōs looking at her with so much love that his eyes seemed to blaze with a blinding light.

For a moment neither of them could move.

Then, as Thea felt that she must be dreaming, King Árpád said,

"I have something important to tell Your Majesties and perhaps it would be possible for me to do so alone."

Thea's father looked at him in surprise and asked him,

"Could it not wait until after luncheon?"

"It will take only a few minutes," King Árpád replied, "and, if perhaps we could go into another room with Her Majesty and your daughter I can tell you why I am here."

Thea was aware that her father was thinking that this was all very unconventional.

There was, however, nothing that he could do but lead the way into an anteroom that led off the salon. It was a small room that Thea had always thought was one of the prettiest in The Palace.

The door was closed behind them and King Árpád turned to Thea and held out his hand.

She moved towards him with the swiftness of a small bird seeking safety.

Her heart was beating excitedly and at the same time she was feeling bewildered and could scarcely believe that it was really Nikōs who stood there in front of her.

Nikōs, looking so tall and so regal and so very much a King, but also the man who she was married to.

He held Thea's hand very firmly in his and then he said in a low voice,

"I told you to trust me!"

It was impossible for her to speak, but from the way she looked up at him it was obvious that she loved him.

Then he turned to her father,

"I came here today, Your Majesty, to tell you, although you may find it hard to believe, that Thea and I were married four days ago!"

The King stared at him as if he thought that he could not be hearing him correctly.

Then the Queen exclaimed,

"*Married*? But how is it possible?"

"We met in the wood," Nikōs explained, "and we fell in love. Thea had no idea who I was and I had no idea who she was, but we knew that we were part of each other and nothing else was of any significance."

"This is the most extraordinary story I have ever heard!" the King declared.

Thea saw, however, that he did not seem to be angry.

She knew that his astonishment was tempered by the knowledge that King Árpád ruled over a country that was far larger and more important than Kostas.

In point of fact he could not have asked for a more prestigious son-in-law.

Now Nikōs was saying,

"That is the real reason, but there is another one, one that will convince the world why we were married."

Thea looked at him a little apprehensively.

He told her father and mother how, having met, they were riding in the woods when they had been captured by the bandits.

He explained that, in order to save Thea from the unwelcome attention of the younger bandits, he had told them that they were married. And they had therefore left her alone.

The Queen gave an exclamation of horror, while Thea's father said,

"That was very clever of you and I am certainly extremely grateful that you saved my daughter from those brutes."

"Fortunately," Nikōs went on, "whenever I am living incognito at my little house in the mountains, which I had built myself so that I could enjoy my painting undisturbed, my Prime Minister has always been insistent, although I would not be aware of it, that I am watched in case of any attack on me."

"So I should hope," the King commented. "You are far too important to be left alone and unattended."

"It was something that I have resented and tried to forget," Nikōs replied, "but on this occasion I was very grateful."

He looked at Thea lovingly as he went on,

"My invisible guard saw me being taken away, but he would have been powerless to tackle the bandits by himself even with the soldier who was with him. He therefore notified the nearest detachment of troops who came to our rescue as soon as it was dawn."

The Queen gave a little cry of horror.

"I cannot bear to think of the danger you were in."

"Nor I," the King said. "How can Thea have been so naughty as to run away in that reckless fashion?"

Thea smiled at him.

"Are you not glad now, Papa, that I did so? If I had stayed here, I would never have found Nikōs."

"I imagine that is one of your many names," the King remarked to Nikōs.

"I have five of them," Nikōs smiled.

"I have three!" Thea interposed.

"I am quite content with the one you use," he remarked quietly.

The two Kings then decided that they would announce that Nikōs had met Thea when she had been captured by bandits.

He had saved her and in doing so they had fallen in love.

"It is a story that our people will greatly enjoy," the Queen said, "and I am so happy those horrible creatures are behind bars and no longer able to threaten travellers or steal our livestock."

"You may be sure of that," Nikōs said.

They then went back to the salon and as they did so he said,

"I will look after Thea now and prevent her from having such risky adventures in the future."

*

There was no chance of their being alone until late in the afternoon when Thea asked him,

"Why did you not tell me?"

"Why did you not tell *me*!" Nikōs riposted.

"I-I was afraid," Thea confessed, "that you would not marry me – if you knew how – angry my father would be and that I would be – stripped of my rank for having married a – commoner."

She gave a little cry as she pressed herself against him saying,

"How could I have known – how could I have guessed that – you were so Royal?"

Nikōs's lips were on her forehead as he said,

"I did not tell you, my darling, because I was afraid that you might be insulted at having a morganatic marriage."

Thea looked up at him in astonishment.

"Morganatic marriage?" she questioned.

"I went to my Palace yesterday to inform my Prime Minister that I was married and to ask if they would accept someone as beautiful and as perfect as my wife and their Queen."

He gave a sigh as he added,

"I knew that it would be very difficult."

"Why?" Thea asked.

"Because my Cabinet, my family and everybody from the shoemaker to the blacksmith, who I rule over, have all been nagging me and begging me to marry and have an heir for several years now."

"And I thought you were an artist!"

Nikōs laughed.

"I went off by myself to paint simply to find a little peace and so I was determined that I would not have an arranged marriage to some plain boring Princess just to please the people."

"Is that what I am?" Thea asked.

He turned her small face up to his with his finger and said,

"You know what I feel about you and I will make it even plainer a little later."

The touch of his finger made her feel as if there was a little flame touching her skin, but she forced herself to ask him,

"But you did not tell – your Prime Minister that you were – married to me. Why not?"

Nikōs smiled.

"The bandits did me a good turn."

"The bandits? But – how?"

"When I came back to The Palace, the Officer who had taken your saddle to be mended asked to see me."

He smiled again before he went on,

"He told me in a serious tone that he thought I ought to know that the saddle had been stolen from the Royal stables at Gyula!"

"But of course!" Thea exclaimed. "Papa's Coat of Arms is always marked somewhere on the saddles!"

"Exactly," Nikōs agreed. "And that is how I found out who I was married to."

"You were – sure of it?"

"I had been continually told that Princess Sydel was very beautiful. My Prime Minister and most of my family had practically gone on their knees to beg me to meet you, but I had always declined."

"But – why?"

"Because I was waiting for the right woman who belonged to me and who was the other half of myself," Nikōs said quietly. "And I felt sure that Héja would send her to me sooner or later."

"And that is what he did!"

Then she gave a little laugh.

"How could I have guessed when I fell over you and thought that you were an artist that you were a King as well?"

"I thought that you were a Goddess or a nymph from the lake," Nikōs replied, "but all that mattered was that you were mine and I had waited a very long time for you."

As he spoke, he kissed her.

Then, as they clung together, Thea thought that all her Fairytales had come true.

She had found her Prince Charming. She was the other half of him as he was the other half of her.

They were together and now nothing could ever separate them.

*

Later that night when they were together in the largest and grandest State room in The Palace, Thea asked,

"How can we be so lucky – so incredibly and marvellously lucky – to be here – together tonight?"

"I think the answer to that," Nikōs said seriously, "is that we have faith in our own ideals and our belief in real true love."

He pulled her a little closer before he continued,

"It was that which made you run away from the thought of being married to King Otho. It was because I knew you were somewhere out there in the world, if only I could find you, that I escaped from the pomp and protocol of The Palace to my little house in the woods."

He moved his lips over her skin before he said,

"I thought about you when I was painting the walls of my bedroom and I was actually thinking of you when I was painting the lake where we met."

"You have to finish that picture," Thea insisted.

"We are going there to continue our honeymoon as soon as you have seen my Palace and met my family."

"Can we really go there and just have Valou and his wife to look after us?"

"We will be invisibly protected," Nikōs answered gravely. "I would never risk your precious life again, my darling, but to all intents and purposes we shall be completely alone."

"Oh, Nikōs, that is just what I want. I want to sleep in your butterfly bed and ride with you to the little Church to thank the Priest who made me your wife."

"We will do all those things," he said, "but most of all, my beloved darling, I will make you love me more than you do already."

"That is impossible!"

Yet, as his hand touched her body, she felt a wild thrill moving like fire from her breast to her lips.

She knew now that she was loving him more than she had done yesterday or indeed the day before.

It was a Love that would grow and intensify not only on their honeymoon but for the rest of their lives.

It was a Love that came from God, a love too that was an intricate part of the mountains, the flowers, the music of the gypsies, the butterflies and the birds.

It was a Love that they would give to their children and to all those whom they ruled over.

Without Love the world was empty.

With Love it was filled with sunshine and fire and the stars, which were in themselves the Light of God.

OTHER BOOKS IN THIS SERIES

The Barbara Cartland Eternal Collection is the unique opportunity to collect all five hundred of the timeless beautiful romantic novels written by the world's most celebrated and enduring romantic author.

Named the Eternal Collection because Barbara's inspiring stories of pure love, just the same as love itself, the books will be published on the internet at the rate of four titles per month until all five hundred are available.

The Eternal Collection, classic pure romance available worldwide for all time.